A Rachel Markham Mystery

THE MARBURY MURDERS
BOOK 5 - IN THE MYSTERY SERIES

A Rachel Markham Mystery

THE MARBURY MURDERS
BOOK 5 - IN THE MYSTERY SERIES

P.B. KOLLERI

Notion Press

Copyright © P.B Kolleri 2015

All Rights Reserved.

ISBN: 978-15-11655-22-4

Dedicated to my partner in life and crime,
The decidedly better, calmer and saner half of the Kolleris...
This one is for you.

The shaft of the arrow had been feathered with one
of the eagle's own plumes.
We often give our enemies the means of our own destruction.

~ Aesop, The Eagle and the Arrow, 560 BC

Chapter One

Marbury Hall. England.

Boxing Day 1947.

The foxhunt had begun in earnest as the storm clouds gathered ominously overhead. A little further up from the woods, a relentlessly cold wind whipped around the lonely hill top, as the Earl of Marbury cantered up and turned his horse around on the grassy knell. From here he had a spectacular view of his estate.

A handsome man in his early fifties, Lord Marbury was blessed with genes that defied his age. A full head of salt and pepper hair under his riding hat only added intrigue to his classical good looks, which were enhanced by a square jaw, an athletic build and deep grey eyes that shone with humour on most days. The earl had detached himself from the throng of riders and made his way to his favourite spot, just after the hunting party had entered the woods. He did enjoy hosting the hunt, the house party and the traditional fanfare involving the call to hounds and the horns at dawn but that was where his interest in foxhunting began and ended.

Having succeeded to the title and the estates that came with it, after the three heirs ahead of him succumbed to their untimely deaths twenty years ago, it was understandable that unlike the others, he did not enjoy the pleasurable blood sport of his titled cousins and ancestors. In his youth he had been content to be a debonair young man about town and through the remainder of his adult life he had preferred a different sort of sport altogether, which ironically also involved a chase of sorts. He was a lover of all things beautiful and had quite a reputation with the ladies. Foxhunting was simply not his thing and deep in his heart he echoed the views of one of Oscar Wilde's characters who described it, tongue-in-cheek, as *'the unspeakable in full pursuit of the uneatable',* although he would rather drop dead than admit the fact in public. His horse, Painter, on the other hand was a thoroughly well-bred aristocrat keen for the hunt.

As man and beast stood atop the hill, Lord Marbury took in the myriad shades of greys and greens of the panoramic view on offer and felt a sense of deep satisfaction of a man who has come a long way to finally find that he is indeed the King of all he surveys. Thunder rumbled across his land and drowned the sounds of the hunt that emanated from the woods below. He could see the majestic ramparts of his home – Marbury Hall from his perch and once again felt awash with the wonder of it all. Never in a million years had he thought that life would present such a gift to him.

Exactly twenty years ago, in one fell twist of fate, he, erstwhile Mr. Magnus Pelham, the youngest partner at the London solicitor's firm of Gordon, Waddington and Davis, had gone overnight from being a relatively unknown nobody to becoming the Earl of Marbury and all that it entailed – wealth beyond measure, several townhouses in London, Paris, Vienna, two picturesque villas – one in Monte Carlo and another in Rome, and the jewel of the inheritance – Marbury Hall. The latter was one of the most coveted country estates in England, which boasted a magnificent Elizabethan structure surrounded by thousands of acres of farms, lush meadow land and woods, which became his along with the Earl's coronet.

He sighed contentedly. Life had been good to him. Post-war years had been hard on everybody, but after the first war he had strived to modernise the farm equipment and integrate tenant farmers into viewing farming as an industry. They had started scientific crop rotation, merged the smaller farms to develop larger tracts of land for cash crops and separated the meadows for animal husbandry. At the time, a lot of his titled peers had turned their noses up at what they perceived was his 'middle class' working mindset. They had pooh-poohed his revolutionary ideas that the old estates could not possibly go on the way they had for hundreds of years previously. Now after the added economic devastation of the Second World War, parallel estates and age old aristocratic homes were dissolving like salt crystals in water across the land. Reeling under financial duress, the same detractors had grudgingly accepted the validity of his views and some had begun to give him the tag of a 'visionary'.

The estates at Marbury Hall had finally become self sustaining after a decade and half of gradual yet effective modernisation. Finally the years of hard work and industry were paying off. Marbury Hall had earned the glistening reputation of being one of the few grand aristocratic seats in England that had not only survived but flourished despite the wages of war. So much so that despite being a Labour leader, the Prime Minister Clement Attlee had invited him to 10 Downing on several occasions to garner his support and ask for his help to form a committee for rehabilitating the surviving aristocratic estates, which were on the verge of crumbling across England. It was also common knowledge that the leader of opposition, the erstwhile Prime Minister, Winston Churchill himself was on a first name basis with him and spent several weekends enjoying Lord Marbury's hospitality at Marbury Hall.

Looking back over the years, Lord Marbury had the satisfaction of acknowledging that he had always had a good head for business and had made a resounding success of it all. But life was full of ironies and surprises. And now after all these years, his forgotten past had come back to haunt him. But he would not let it defeat him. Like everything else in his life he knew exactly how to turn a challenge into an opportunity.

Suddenly in the midst of his calm reminisces, a deafening shot rang out from behind a clump of bushes forty yards to his right and startled both the rider and the horse, the latter of which reared up and made a dash for it, while the former felt a searing pain burn through his head. The gunshot was the last thing Lord Marbury heard before he fell to the ground.

II

Twenty minutes later, in the luxuriously appointed morning room of Marbury Hall, the Countess being an early riser had dutifully seen off the hunting party, and was now busy sipping her morning tea and tackling her correspondence. She was a well proportioned woman in her late forties with masses of unruly blonde hair that kept escaping the prison of numerous hairpins, and found their way regularly into her sea blue eyes. Brushing aside the stray locks from her face had almost become a mannerism for her. The more Tilly – her diligent lady's maid tried to discipline her locks into some sort of fashionable styling, the further freedom they sought. That however did not prevent Tilly – the ever optimistic maid to continue fighting a failing battle on a daily basis. She was proud of her mistress and extremely pleased about the fact that twenty years ago, she had been promoted overnight from being a grubby little parlour maid to becoming a lady's maid to the Countess of Marbury.

By all accounts the Countess of Marbury – erstwhile Catherine Pelham nee Sommerville was considered a great beauty. Despite her week chin, a slightly flat nose and an undeniably sheepish profile, her features came together in a manner that was altogether pleasing to the eye. People who knew her well attributed her beauty to the quality of goodness that shone out through her smiling countenance and reached her clear blue eyes. At the moment she was engrossed in replying to a letter from a friend in America.

Despite the crackling log fire in the room, she felt a momentary chill as though someone had just walked over her bones. She shuddered as she put her fountain pen down and then looked out the window. She could hear the thunder interspersed by the rumble of a thousand dark clouds that had seemed to roll over from nowhere and covered the clear blue sky of the past week. Up until yesterday they had had unusually good weather for this time of year. She was thankful for that. To her mind there was nothing worse than inclement weather. And nothing more tedious than trying to devise ways and means of keeping a large house party amused indoors.

The big house was unusually silent. She wondered about it. She knew that the servants were probably taking their breakfast in the servant's hall downstairs. Of her remaining house guests who had not joined the hunt, the married ladies would still be asleep or be taking their breakfast in bed. Her two unmarried daughters, Lady Claire and Lady Stephanie were probably still asleep and would come down in a while to partake theirs in the family's dining hall along with the others who had not felt equal to rising this early to participate in the foxhunt.

She smiled as she thought of her girls. Claire was twenty two and Stephanie had just turned twenty last month. She was proud of the fact that unlike herself at their age, her daughters were headstrong young ladies with a mind of their own. She also took satisfaction in the fact that Claire was affianced to Neville Pelham, who was next in line to the Earldom. Such a sensible young woman Claire had turned out to be.

She had no doubt that her younger daughter Stephanie would make a brilliant match as well when the time came. Already young Roddy Cartwright, the only son and heir of Baron Braybourne was taking quite an interest in her. The fact that theirs was one of the wealthiest and oldest baronies in the land only made the match seem that much sweeter in the Countess' maternal albeit calculating mind.

The young members of the party were a boisterous lot and Tilly had informed her this morning that the girls and some of the younger guests had continued the spirit of Christmas celebrations by staying up for the better part of the night, dancing to records played on the gramophone.

As she finished writing the last of her letters, she heard voices in the hall and a door bang somewhere and decided with a sigh that she would ask her girls to join her in the morning room if they were up, and request them to come up with some games to keep everyone amused for the rest of the day. She rang the bell pull.

Shortly the door opened and instead of Hobbs, the butler, whom she was expecting, in came her sister, Miranda Sommerville. Miranda was an antithesis to her. She was only two years younger than herself but had never married. Instead she had chosen to spend the better part of her adult life in Kenya, purportedly doing good deeds and helping out at the mission run by her friends, the Reverend Peter and Felicity Brabazon at Nairobi. She was wearing riding breeches that accentuated her tall, slim boyish figure. Her complexion was dark owing to the tan accumulated over the years spent under the African Sun. Unlike her sister, she had a youthful look, shingled dark hair and on normal days, flashing brown eyes which shone with intelligence. At the moment they had a wild expression in them and she was looking quite agitated whilst uncharacteristically wringing her hands.

'What's the matter, Miranda? Has anything happened?' The Countess asked getting up from her chair in concern.

'It has rather. I thought I should be the one to tell you. Magnus has been shot. The boys have just telephoned the doctor and the police but...'

Before she could finish, the Countess of Marbury had let out a muffled cry and collapsed on the thick carpet in a dead faint.

'Oh, bother!' Miranda mumbled to herself and raised an eyebrow at the human heap in front of her. She then calmly walked to the door and hollered, 'Hobbs! Get some smelling salts! Better yet get Tilly! Now, if you please!'

Chapter Two

A week later, Chief Inspector Harrow of Scotland Yard was motoring back to London after concluding preliminary investigations in the case up at Marbury Hall. He stopped at Marbury Arms and made a telephone call. The call resulted in his taking a fifty mile detour off the road back to London, to pay a call on Jeremy Richards and his wife Rachel at Rutherford Hall. He hoped it would be worth it. He was in a quandary and the first solution that came to his mind was to enlist the couple in question to help him overcome a tricky situation.

Jeremy Richards and the Chief Inspector went back a long way, over two decades by their mutual association with Scotland Yard. Despite being one of the toffs with his gentlemanly bearing and a wealthy public school upbringing, Jeremy Richards had turned out to be one of his best men. Harrow smiled as he remembered his surprise when he first heard what the others at the Yard had nicknamed this dignified, tall and good looking man - the *bull terrier*. And with good reason. He had been unstoppable to the point of being relentless when he was on the trail of a killer. And he always got his man. For two long decades, the outwardly unassuming Richards had had an exemplary career in law enforcement and had created a formidable reputation for himself at the Yard. That was before the terrible Archer murder case. *God awful case*, Harrow thought to himself as his smile faded and he recalled the turning point in Richards' life and career.

It had involved the death of a nine year old schoolboy, Percy Archer who had inadvertently witnessed a murder and had in turn become the next victim of the ruthless and sadistic murderer. Richards had not only uncovered the truth that the murderer was a high profile politician and peer, but had also completely ignored the hush orders that had then been put on the case from the highest political echelons. Upon finding the tortured and mutilated body of the small child in the woods, he had gone ahead and meted out his own form of justice on Lord Heatherton, the peer in question, hush orders be damned.

Although Harrow understood how deeply Richards had been affected by the visible brutal torture and physical abuse the child had undergone before he was killed, he could not condone the fact that Richards had deliberately gone out of line and beaten up the accused, Lord Heatherton, almost to death. It would have undoubtedly led to severe disciplinary action against Richards, if he hadn't been winged by Heatherton's gun and claimed that he had acted out of self defence. Despite the support from his colleagues owing to the far more heinous nature of Lord Heatherton's crimes, the establishment had still come down hard on Scotland Yard, baying for blood.

Richards of course, in his own way, had saved them all a great deal of embarrassment by voluntarily opting for early retirement. But it had been a dark day for Chief Inspector Harrow, who knew without a doubt that Scotland Yard had lost one of her finest men, the day the *bull terrier* had walked away from it all, with a blemished reputation to supposedly lead a quiet life in the country.

But life has a strange way of coming a full circle and Jeremy Richards was flung back into law enforcement, albeit of a different kind, by force of circumstances. He had not only been responsible for finding the culprit in the Rutherford Hall murder case with the help of Lord Rutherford's niece, Rachel Markham but had also found a mate in her. Harrow smiled once more as he thought of young Rachel. Harrow was good at sussing out people and he knew without a doubt that in Rachel, Jeremy Richards – the erstwhile confirmed old bachelor had finally found his match. Chief Inspector Harrow soon cottoned on to the fact that despite her outward appearance of being a fashionable and flighty young lady, she had formidable intelligence and crime solving capabilities in her own right.

Over the past year and a half Jeremy and Rachel had gone on to solve complex murder cases and had earned the reputation of being one of the finest teams in the arena of private criminal investigations. So much so that three months ago, on the Chief Inspector's personal recommendation, they had been invited by an Indian Maharajah to solve a murder case and a jewel heist that had taken place in a princely state in British India, which they had successfully unravelled. Post which, they wrapped up yet another case on their way back from India, on their stopover at Paris, which involved the murder of Countess Santinelli – an international celebrity and one of the wealthiest women in the world.

Their reputation had now grown on an international scale. Recently returned from Paris, and ensconced once more at Rutherford Hall, the Chief Inspector knew instinctively that if this case at Marbury Hall was baffling enough to arouse Rachel's curiosity, it would be sufficient bait to rope them both in. After a fruitless week of full-fledged police investigations at Marbury Hall, he had no qualms in admitting that he could certainly use their help. He needed trustworthy moles on the inside if he were to get to the bottom of this, people who could seamlessly fit into a plush country house setting and join the high profile house party without arousing too much suspicion. To his mind, Rachel and Jeremy fit the bill perfectly.

II

'Happy New Year, Chief Inspector. How wonderful to see you again,' Rachel said, as she walked across the oak panelled library at Rutherford Hall to greet her guest.

'Likewise, my dear. I hear you've been keeping Richards on his toes. First India, then Paris,' the Chief Inspector said with a smile in Rachel's direction as he shook hands with Jeremy.

Rachel replied with a grin, 'You've got it the other way round, Chief Inspector! He's the one who takes all the decisions. I simply tag along as the meek and obedient wife.'

Jeremy smiled as he retorted, 'Yes, and I am quite certain that anyone who knows you, my darling, would have no trouble whatsoever in believing that.' Then turning to Harrow, he said, 'It is always good to see you, Chief Inspector. To what do we owe this pleasure?'

'Ah, well, yes... you were always one of the best, Richards. Take a wild guess,' Harrow said with a sheepish smile.

'I am hoping beyond hope, Sir, that this has nothing to do with the recent incident up at Marbury Hall.'

'Then I am sorry to disappoint you. At any rate I'm glad to see you haven't lost your touch,' Harrow said.

Jeremy responded. 'Thank you. Sad business about the shooting though. We read about it in the papers. Do you think he'll pull through?'

'It's early days yet. I'd like to say where there's life, there's hope and all that sort of thing but I doubt it. He's still in a coma and the doctor informed me this morning that although his vital signs are improving post surgery, his condition remains critical. Considering one of the pellets was lodged in the frontal lobe of his brain, I'm surprised he's lasted this long.'

Rachel interjected, 'How awful. Any ideas on who shot him?'

'Not yet, I'm afraid. The process is beginning to look more and more like searching for a needle in a haystack.'

Rachel nodded. 'From what I've read in the papers, it was quite a large haystack. A house party of thirty five not counting the additional headcount of the guest's servants – maids, valets, chauffeurs and so on.'

'Quite!'

Rachel spoke. 'But surely they can't all be staying on indefinitely after the attempted murder?'

Harrow replied. 'Well, I've allowed most of the guests to leave this morning. I had no choice. After all, it has been a week since the incident and as you mentioned we can't ask the guests to stay on forever at Marbury Hall. Some of them are key political figures and heads of industry. They do have lives to lead and business interests to go back to.'

'But won't that hamper your investigation?' Rachel queried.

Harrow replied. 'That is the trouble, you see. I spent most of last week along with the local constabulary, interrogating the lot of them and we've gotten absolutely nowhere. As you know it isn't exactly a murder investigation – well not as yet. Though I am quite sure that someone up there has murderous intentions and is in all likelihood planning to finish what he started. I have a sense of foreboding but my hands are tied; I've been recalled to another urgent case at the Yard. As you are aware, we've been terribly shorthanded since the war. For the time being I've asked the local police to continue the investigation but I'm afraid...'

Jeremy interjected, 'Say no more. We understand perfectly. Is there anyone in particular from the house party that you suspect? Perhaps someone with a political motive, a houseguest or a family member?'

'Yes and no. Most of the men were accounted for anyway by the others at the hunt. Aside from the family members and guests who stayed back, we also questioned everyone who was at the hunt, including the hunt master, the whippers-in and the servants. No one in the fox hunting party was carrying any weapon of any sort, leave alone a shotgun – a weapon that is not easy to conceal on one's person unlike a revolver. And nobody seems to have noticed anything untoward until they heard the gunshot and spotted the Lordship's horse galloping down the hill without the rider.'

Jeremy asked, 'The shotgun could have easily been planted near the hill before the hunt started. Do you know why Lord Marbury left the hunt to go up the hill? Was it to meet someone?'

'I haven't the foggiest notion. He's been in a coma ever since. We did not find any note on his person or in his room to suggest a proposed meeting. But there is the possibility that the murderer may have removed it after he shot the Earl. But I can tell you that whoever shot him was on foot because there were only one set of fresh hoof prints near the spot, which belonged to his Lordship's horse.'

Rachel asked, 'Any identifiable footprints?'

'Dozens! A lot of people went up the hill to look for him after they spotted the rider-less horse flying down the hill. Probably obliterating the murderer's prints while they were at it. Also, people did take long walks all over the estate during the house party and the hill was a scenic spot.'

Rachel nodded. 'Hmm. The papers said he was shot with a 12 bore shotgun. A woman could have shot him just as easily as a man.'

'Yes but in my experience a shotgun is typically a man's weapon. Women tend to employ subtler methods and prefer smaller weapons; knives, hand guns, poison...'

Jeremy nodded. 'I have to agree there.'

Rachel rolled her eyes, 'It may have escaped your notice, gentlemen, but the world is changing as we speak; as far as women are concerned. The war saw to that. So, if I were you, I wouldn't overlook the possibility that a woman could have committed this crime.'

The Chief Inspector nodded. 'I suppose you could be right. Either way, it means it could have been anyone, more likely someone from the house. There is no dearth of shotguns in the Castle's well appointed gun room. Although as clumsy as it may sound, despite forensic reports and gun residue tests, it looks like the chap...er... person who did this, was careful enough to get rid of the gun and the gloves he or she wore. We have not been able to zero in on the guilty weapon yet.'

Jeremy, who had been listening intently so far, finally spoke. 'I think under the circumstances, if as you suspect, a member of the Earl's house party is behind this and especially if the evidence has since been obliterated, the best way to go about it from this point on would be to plant undercover agents at Marbury Hall. It may help you figure out the motive behind the crime and zero in on possible suspects and who stands to gain most if His Lordship succumbs to his injuries.'

Harrow smiled. 'Precisely. Which brings me to you two.'

Jeremy shook his head in disbelief, 'Oh, no...not again. We just got back. And given Lord Marbury's high profile, I was thinking more on the lines of MI5...'

Harrow sighed. 'I'm afraid, thanks to the war most MI5 operatives have been inducted into the MI6 and are currently engaged in operations across the world, notably in India, Burma and Ceylon. These are tumultuous times we live in, Richards. Between you and me, there are rumours of trouble brewing in Cyprus and Malaya. Word has it that we are also in the process of wrapping up the Palestine Mandate. Not to mention the new military base we are building in Kenya. I'm sure you'll agree that there is far too much happening in the world at the moment for the remaining intelligence operatives to warrant attention on a single, near fatal shooting incident.'

Jeremy nodded gloomily and Rachel's eyes lit up as she said, 'I'm sure we'd like to help, but how do *we* go about it?'

Harrow smiled. 'Well, at the risk of sounding terribly presumptuous, I've already had a word with the Countess who is keen to aid in the investigation, in any way she can. And upon my request she has issued an open invitation to you both, to join what's left of the house party at Marbury Hall,' he said searching through his jacket pockets and bringing out a folded card.

Rachel took it and said, 'Oh, my! This is a surprise. And when are we supposed to join in?'

Harrow answered, 'Well, it is up to you really. I did tell her that it would depend on how you both were placed at this busy time of year and that I would let her know should you wish to accept her invitation. Needless to add; I am hoping that you will.'

Jeremy answered slowly, 'Well, despite my reservations, if Rachel is up to it, I think we ought to. I have a great deal of respect and admiration for a visionary like Lord Marbury. I should hate to think that the chap who did this, is at this very moment, sitting somewhere and smugly contemplating that he got away with a dastardly crime.'

Chapter Three

Neville Pelham was in the library at Marbury Hall contemplating his future prospects, which seemed somewhat brighter at the moment. He was all said and done, next in line to inherit the Earldom. He hoped that his creditors would back down for now and give him some much needed breathing space. Some of the less tenacious ones had been placated once his betrothal to Lady Claire had been announced in The Times a month ago. But he still cringed at the thought of the toughs that Albert Simmons, Esquire – book keeper to the titled, had conscientiously sent to take up temporary residence at Marbury Arms, the local public house and inn.

Both the toughs were ex-boxers and had accosted him two weeks ago, when he was trying to quietly drown his financial sorrows in a pint of bitter at the pub. They had proceeded to inform him that they were there to keep an eye on him and generally make his life a tad more miserable than it had been up until now. And his only hope, Lord Marbury had very emphatically turned down his umpteenth plea for financial aid. Of course now things would be different, he thought to himself given that the relatively young and fit Lord Marbury had done him a favour of immense magnitude by being at the receiving end of an almost fatal shot.

As Neville felt sorry about all he had to endure for the past year, the door opened and the parlour maid, 'Summer' came in carrying a tea tray. She was a buxom country girl, with green eyes and curly blonde locks, which were artfully arranged to escape her white maid's cap. There was something undeniably fresh about her face. The uncharitable would put down her fresh appeal to the first flush of youth but in Neville's eyes, he was yet to see another that could match her charms. Even in her unbecoming black uniform and the starched white apron, he found her womanly curves irresistible. His face lit up and he got up and walked over to her. She in turn smiled back at him coquettishly, set down the tray on the nearest table and then turned to face him.

Neville spoke with relief in his voice. 'Thank God you found me alone for once, my darling. I could use a kiss right about now,' he said, as he took her willing body into his arms and their lips locked in a passionate kiss. A moment later there was a sound at the door and they hastily separated. Luckily, no one had entered but it was enough for the lovers to exercise caution and start whispering.

Neville looked into her eyes and whispered, 'I wish we didn't have to resort to skulduggery all the time.'

Summer gave a nervous giggle and responded, 'How long do you think it'll be before I have to start addressing you as "Milord"?'

He answered gloomily. 'I really couldn't say, my darling. I thought it was going to be smooth sailing from here on but Dr. Farnsworth, blast the man, informed me quite cheerfully this very morning that he's come across cases where people have lived on for years and years in a comatose state!'

'Oh, dear, that does put us in a fix. Father isn't going to like my carrying on with you, now that you're engaged to Lady Claire. He says you're just foolin' around with me. He's already started warning me off you. If I were you, I'd watch my step around him, luv.'

Neville shuddered as he had a momentary vision of Summer's father, Bill Hogan – the well built and often disgruntled gamekeeper of Marbury Hall giving him chase with a shotgun or some other weapon in hand.

He looked at her fearfully and said in a placating voice, 'Yes, but you know the engagement is just eyewash to keep off the bloody creditors. There's nothing between me and Lady Claire.' Then brightening up as an idea came to him, he said, 'I say, why don't you meet me at our usual place tonight?'

'Hmph! And I'm just supposed to go on making myself available to you whenever you get an itch, am I?' Was her unromantic reply.

'What do you want me to do, Summer? It's not like we can dash off and get married with things being the way they are!'

'But we can. Remember I told you about what I found amongst my poor dead mother's things. All I have to do is get my hands on the money and we can lead our lives the way we want. It may not be as grand as all this, I s'ppose, but you'll get used to it.'

'You don't know what you're asking me to do. I have a role to play here. I am going to be the next Earl.'

'That's right. You just sit around here, waiting till you're old, waiting for his Lordship to kick the bucket before you can start livin' your own life.'

'You are not being fair. Please, give me time to think. I promise I'll consider your proposal.'

'Well don't make me wait forever. And you had better make up your mind soon or you'll have me dad to answer to, and that won't be all that pleasant, as sweet as my old man is.'

At this point Neville made a gurgling sound very much like a frog who had just spotted a snake slithering towards him with a gleam in its eye that gave the impression that it no longer needs to worry about its next meal. Not for the first time in his life he found himself in an awkward spot. Sweet old man, indeed!

He was saved from responding to Summer's veiled threats as the door opened and Lady Claire walked in. She was a tall slim brunette who had her father's deep grey eyes which gave her a certain personality. One could not call her pretty but she had a commanding presence, a rare quality in someone so young that it made people look at her twice even if they were simply passing her on the street.

This admirable quality however made Neville shiver in his boots at the very thought of what his future nuptials might bring if he didn't think fast of some way to get out of the mess he was in. He far preferred the rustic charms of sweet buxom Summer, even though her bleating had gone up a notch lately.

Lady Claire addressed Neville. 'There you are, my dear. I've been looking for you everywhere,' she said, as she came and gave him a peck on his cheek. Then turning to Summer who was still rooted to the spot, she asked imperiously, 'Are you still here? Don't you have some trays to carry or beds to turn down?'

'Yes, milady.'

'Then I suggest you stop haunting the library and get on with it.'

'Yes, milady,' she curtsied and backed off, giving Neville a parting glare.

Once she was out the door, Summer put her back against the closed door and as there was no one around, she allowed a smug smile to spread across her face. She'd show the high and mighty Lady Claire what was what once she, the lowly parlour maid had all the money in the world and had bagged Neville Pelham for a husband. Then her smug smile faded as a more worrying thought occurred to her. She decided to go back to her room at the gamekeeper's cottage and find a safer hiding place for the things she had found – the things that would lead her to her envisioned pot of gold and better yet, life-long freedom from drudgery.

On the other side of the door, Neville spoke, 'Must you be so rude to the staff?'

'I don't know what you are talking about! The staff loves me. That parlour maid just gets my back up. Have you noticed, she's been giving herself a lot of airs lately? And Tilly is always ticking her off. I think I'll have a word with Mama and have the girl sacked. We can't have Tilly upset. '

Neville just stood there and gurgled some more.

Lady Claire then proceeded to make herself comfortable in an armchair near the tea tray and poured herself some tea. Then as an afterthought she asked, 'Don't you want tea?'

Neville shook his head. What he really wanted was a strong shot of whiskey. And since that was not currently on offer, he picked up a cucumber sandwich and started munching on it listlessly.

Lady Claire continued, 'Oh, and have you heard? Mama says we are going to have private detectives in the house.'

'Eh, what? What on earth do we need detectives nosing about here for? I thought Scotland Yard was on the case.'

'Oh, they are. Mama says the Chief Inspector from the Yard himself suggested that these detectives be brought in. From what I gather, it's all very hush-hush. So don't dream of breathing a word about it to anyone.'

'But surely you can't be serious? Why would we need more people nosing about at a time like this! Where will they stay?'

'Oh, here of course. Mama says they are perfectly respectable and practically aristocracy. In fact she told me that the lady detective is the erstwhile Lord Rutherford's niece. And her husband was a high ranking inspector who worked with the Yard for years. They are to stay here ostensibly as our house guests while they conduct their investigation.'

'But dash it! Detectives in the house? Are we all to be treated as criminals? I don't fancy the idea one bit.'

'There's no use arguing, darling. Mama has sent Stephanie with the chauffeur to receive them at the station. They ought to be here any minute so you had better get used to the idea even if you don't fancy it.'

Chapter Four

Rachel and Jeremy had reached Marbury Hall just in time to freshen up and change for dinner. As they came down at the sound of the first gong, they were ushered into the plush sitting room for a round of cocktails. They found they were early and only two ladies were seated on a settee at the far end of the room near the log fire. While the Countess was in a light grey evening gown accessorised with diamonds, the other lady was simply dressed in a white silk shirt and a long navy blue skirt. She wore no makeup or jewellery. Rachel was glad she herself had dressed sensibly in a black and white Chanel gown with just a string of pearls around her throat.

The Countess of Marbury stood up and came forward to greet them with a warm smile. 'I am so glad you both could make it. The others will be joining us soon. Come, let me introduce you to my sister, Miranda

Sommerville. Miranda, this is the couple I was telling you about; Rachel and Jeremy Richards.'

Miranda spoke in her no nonsense way, as she got up and vigorously shook hands with Rachel. 'I am surprised to note that the terrible war despite all its suffering had a silver lining after all; such a liberating effect on women. A lady detective, no less! How fascinating. Catherine has been telling me all about your marvellous exploits. Things were so different when I left for Kenya twenty four years ago.'

'Has it really been that long?' the Countess ventured in a dazed fashion.

Miranda responded. 'You know it has, my dear. Anyhow despite the dreadful circumstances that surround our meeting, I am very honoured to make your acquaintance, my dear.'

Rachel responded warmly, 'That is very kind of you indeed. I do hope we are going to live up to your expectations.'

Miranda said cheerfully, 'The Chief Inspector seems to have no doubt about it, so I don't see any good reason why we should.' Then she turned to shake Jeremy's hand. 'You must be so proud.'

Jeremy shook her hand and smiled in acknowledgement. 'I certainly am but I'm not so sure that the war had much to do with my wife's choice of profession. For as long as I've known her, her ideas have always been like a force of nature; quite unstoppable really. I don't know if I ought to be pleased or worried about it.'

Miranda laughed. 'Pleased to bits, I should hope.'

At that moment an exotic looking, exquisitely gowned lady walked in. Her shimmering silver dress was cut low enough to display her ample charms, a fox fur was stylishly draped on her right shoulder. Her face was heavily made up. What struck Rachel most about her were the large, expressive and liquid eyes which simultaneously captivated and intimidated. She guessed her age to be somewhere in the mid thirties to early forties. She seemed nice enough but as soon as she approached them Rachel could sense a distinct heaviness in the atmosphere, one you could cut with a knife and the bonhomie of the past few moments seemed to have vanished into thin air. She was intrigued by the effect this woman had on the two other ladies present.

The Countess introduced her to them politely with a somewhat forced smile that did not quite reach her eyes. 'This is our guest, Madame Ada Cellini. Ada is a well known soprano and we are proud to be hosting her at Marbury Hall. May I present Rachel and Jeremy Richards.'

Jeremy bowed politely. 'Madame Cellini's reputation precedes her and indeed requires no introduction. We are honoured to make your acquaintance, Madame.'

Ada Cellini spoke in a richly melodious voice. 'Ah! Finally. You are here. Adam informed me you were coming. Now I hope we will learn who was behind this terrible tragedy. My poor, poor Magnus. He of all people did not deserve to be attacked in such a cowardly manner.'

Miranda interjected. 'In what manner would you have preferred that he be attacked, Ada?' She asked in a clipped tone.

Ada Cellini flashed back in anger, 'You are all so unthinking. Is this a time to make your silly English jokes?'

The Countess cut in smoothly, 'I daresay we English have a strange sense of humour but I am quite sure my sister meant no harm. Would you care for a cocktail?' She asked the soprano, as the footman appeared with a drink laden tray supervised by the butler in the background.

'No, I do not care for the cocktails. Or for the dinner. You all behave as though Magnus is merely down with the flu and everything must go on as usual. As though someone did not try to murder him in cold blood. Thoughtless! Thoughtless!' she said dramatically.

Miranda muttered under her breath, 'It certainly didn't prevent you from dressing up like a dog's dinner tonight.' Although she had said it in a very low voice, Rachel overheard and made a heroic attempt to keep a straight face.

Ada Cellini apparently heard it as well as she lost no time in glaring at Miranda and asked, 'What was that?'

Miranda smiled at her sweetly and asked, 'What was what?'

Meanwhile Rachel noticed that the butler whispered something in the Countess' ears as the two walked a few steps away.

The Countess walked back to them and intervened just in time. 'Miranda, my dear, I need to steal you away. Hobbs has just informed me that Dr. Farnsworth is waiting in the library and wants a quick word. You know how hopeless I am with all his new fangled medical terminology. So do excuse us, we shan't be long,' she said to the others, as she guided her sister away from a potentially flammable situation, making a mute appeal in Jeremy's direction as they left.

The exchange between Miranda and Ada Cellini made Rachel wonder at the open animosity they displayed towards each other and she made a swift mental note to find out more about it.

Jeremy came to the rescue. 'Madame Cellini, I think my wife and I were present when you played Tosca at Covent Garden, weren't we darling?'

'Were we?' Rachel asked without thinking.

Jeremy gave Rachel a meaningful glance and continued blithely, 'Yes. Don't you remember? It was such a powerful performance. You said you had never been so moved in your life.'

'Ah, yes I do recall, now that you mention it,' Rachel said as she fell into step with Jeremy's fabrication. 'Madame, you were simply magnificent as Tosca especially in the last death scene when you flung yourself over the parapet and plummeted to your untimely...'

Jeremy gave her a look and interrupted her flow, 'Yes, yes, and of course each and every aria was divine.'

Rachel managed to say with a straight face, 'I have to agree there. Jeremy couldn't stop talking about your performance for days. Made me quite green with envy, I assure you.'

The soprano looked quite pleased for a moment and then her face changed and she sighed and said, 'It is my lifelong burden to bring pleasure to others, while I myself suffer agonies. The past week has been dreadful. Horrible!'

Before either of them could respond to her dramatic statements, two young men in dinner jackets walked into the room. Although they were similarly attired, the contrast between them was like chalk and cheese. The one on the right was deeply tanned, good looking, tall and well-built. He also emanated a good deal of self assurance which in turn made his shorter companion seem somewhat bland and colourless by comparison. Rachel noted that on his own, the man on the left was not bad looking but there was something not quite right about him. Perhaps it was his shifty eyes or his lackadaisical appearance. He seemed to be the sort of man you could meet one day and then instantly forget the next.

Ada Cellini's eyes went to the men, the taller one in particular, and she exclaimed, 'Oh, Adam! Good you are here. Our in-house detectives, the ones you told me about earlier are finally here.'

The way she casually assumed proprietorship over them and the house despite being obviously disliked by the hostess and her sister puzzled Rachel. She put it down to a lack of tact, something one often notices in famous people.

The tall young man however responded to her greeting without any such misgivings and came forward to take her hand with a smile, while his shorter companion walked slowly, two steps behind, licking his lips nervously. He nodded politely to Rachel and Jeremy. The taller of the two introduced himself as Adam Brabazon, and then introduced his companion to them as Neville Pelham.

As they all made polite conversation they were joined by two elegantly dressed young ladies, one of whom Rachel recognised as Lady Stephanie – the younger daughter of the house who had collected them from the station a few hours ago. The tall impressive brunette was introduced to them as her elder sister, Lady Claire. Rachel couldn't help but notice that while Lady Stephanie was small, blonde and talkative, Lady Claire despite her youth had all the makings of a future Countess. And although the sisters were unalike in so many ways, something in the way their features came together made the family resemblance unmistakable.

Lady Stephanie suddenly gave a squeal of delight as a young man with red hair and a freckled face walked into the room. He was wearing a leather jacket and his motoring clothes. 'Roddy! I didn't think you'd be back from London so soon.'

She walked towards him as the young man responded with a smile. 'The Pater let me go early so I drove like the wind to get here just in time. Glad I made it. I'm starved! Sorry I didn't have time to change. I hope the Countess won't fling me out by the ear.'

Stephanie giggled. 'I think she'll overlook it for once given the circs. How is your father?'

'His usual dictatorial self. By the way, he made some vague threats of driving up here tomorrow. Says he wants to personally take another look into this shooting business,' Roddy said with a furrow in his brow.

Stephanie responded with a smile as she took his hand in hers, 'Oh, Roddy, you know he is always welcome here. He and Papa are such good friends. I'll ask Mrs. Simmons to get his usual room ready.'

Roddy nodded and asked, 'Any news from the hospital?'

'Yes. I believe Mama has just stepped out to have a word with Dr. Farnsworth, so we are keeping our fingers crossed. Do come along and meet our guests.' Stephanie smiled as she tugged at his sleeve and introduced him to Rachel and Jeremy as the Honourable Roderick Cartwright.

The Countess and Miranda rejoined them shortly before the second dinner gong went off. They had an announcement. Miranda said they had both good and bad news. The bad news was one of status quo; Lord Marbury was still in a coma. The good news however, was that the doctor had informed them that his condition was not only stable but improving rapidly and that he hoped in due course, his patient would regain consciousness.

Rachel noticed that Jeremy's eyes were scanning the people present to note their reactions to this news. Rachel's gaze fell upon Neville Pelham's face. She fancied she saw a flicker of alarm in his eyes but she could not be sure as within a fraction of a second, she saw a smile on his face as he turned to say something to Lady Claire. Perhaps he was just a tad slow on the uptake, she thought to herself or worse, she had just imagined it. The Chief Inspector had mentioned in his brief that Neville was next in line to inherit and was known to be in financial trouble; facts that may have triggered her imagination. At any rate she decided that she would discuss it with Jeremy the first chance she got to double check if he had noticed it too. Neville certainly needed to be watched more closely.

The prima donna as expected thanked the heavens loudly for showing mercy while the others were more subtle in their expressions of relief that the worst was over. She couldn't help notice that Miranda was the least effusive, but perhaps that was just in bearing with her no-nonsense personality.

Moments later, Hobbs, the stately butler announced that dinner had been served. Adam Brabazon informed Rachel that he had the honour of escorting her in, while Miranda Sommerville took charge of Jeremy. They all walked through to the formal dining room. Given the circumstances, dinner was a subdued affair.

Chapter Five

The next morning Rachel awoke to the sound of a discreet knock as the maid brought in her morning tea and a copy of the Daily Mail. Placing the tray on the small round table near the bed, she then proceeded to open the drapes and silvery sunlight cascaded into the room. Rachel got up and went to the window. Her room was on the first floor and had a wonderful view of the manicured lawns with a large glistening pond in the middle and beyond that to the left were woods that extended as far as the eye could see. The winter fog, which had covered everything on their drive here from the station, had now dissipated and she could see that to the left the landscape extended to the undulating lush green hills. It was a spectacular spot to build a grand house like this.

Whichever Earl built it, Rachel thought to herself, must have returned battle weary and wanted a haven of peace and quiet for a change. Everything looked so serene that it was hard to imagine a place of such calm beauty being associated with violence of any kind. But then the ostentatious display of weaponry, armour and mounted animal heads throughout the house told a story of their own. Rachel was well aware that a great historical title as this and the great wealth associated with it, more often than not, found its origins in rampant bloodshed and the ensuing victories, which went down in history as legendary and were now being taught as history lessons to school children.

As her mind meandered, she realised that the maid was speaking to her.

'I am sorry. What were you saying?'

The maid repeated with thinly veiled impatience that she had been assigned to her as her personal lady's maid for the duration of her stay. She added curtly that she would bring her breakfast tray up shortly.

Rachel told her that it wouldn't be necessary as she preferred to join the others at the breakfast table. The maid shrugged her shoulders sullenly and said, 'As you wish, madam.'

'What is your name?' Rachel asked casually as the maid started tidying up the room. Although she didn't particularly like the girl, Rachel knew that getting to know the staff was the best way to get information out of them. And in most large houses, the staff often held key information that they were unwilling to share with the police.

The maid looked even more sullen as she answered, 'It is Summer, madam.'

'What a nice and unusual name. How long have you worked here, Summer?' She asked with a smile.

Summer stopped what she was doing and her sullen look disappeared to give way to a wan smile as she answered. 'About two months, madam. But I've lived here most of my life. On the grounds that is. My father is the gamekeeper here,' she said with filial pride.

'How lovely. You must enjoy having this position. Saves you the bother of walking to the village for work, I suppose.'

The smile disappeared. 'It is alright, I s'ppose. Though I don't much fancy being a maid for long.' As Rachel raised an eyebrow at this remark, it dawned on Summer that she must have sounded rather rude. She put her hand to her mouth and exclaimed, 'Oh! I am sorry. I shouldn't have said that to you, a guest in the house. Please don't tell on me. There are those who'd like to see the back o'me over here.'

'Really? A nice girl like you? I don't believe it.'

'Not everyone's as nice as you, madam, if I may say so. There are those who are no better than me giving themselves airs as though they were already duchesses here in this house,' she huffed.

'Yes, I'm quite sure it can be a trying experience to please everyone all of the time.'

'It is that, madam. That's as I say to me dad. But he says it's much better to be a maid in a large house than working at a public house or in a factory. But I can tell you it's not much of a life. Oh, dear! I'm doin' it again, aren't I?'

Rachel smiled back and assured the girl. 'Please don't worry on my account. My lips shall remain sealed.'

'It is very kind of you. Most people treat us as though we're furniture. You are kind. Can I get you anything else, madam?' She asked with a genuine smile at having found a kindred soul in Rachel.

'Some more hot water, if it's not too much of a bother. It is rather cold,' Rachel said as she touched the lukewarm jug by the basin.

'Certainly, madam. Be back in a jiffy.'

II

Half an hour later, the sun had come out from behind the clouds and Rachel was enjoying the beautiful view from the dining room windows, which looked out on to the bright sunlit garden. She could see the green hills in the distance. As she munched on delicious hot buttered toast and admired the glorious landscape, Jeremy stepped in through the French windows accompanied by Adam Brabazon.

'Good morning, my dear,' Jeremy greeted her. 'We've just been out for a small walk. Adam was very kindly showing me the lay of the land.'

'How nice for you.' Then turning to Adam, she asked, 'Have you been here long? At Marbury Hall, I mean?'

'Just about two months. I'm organising safari work back in Kenya and Aunt Miranda very kindly got the Countess to put me up, while I had the pleasure of mucking about getting the finances organised and the London end of the outfit up and running.'

'Sounds dreadfully hectic! I wasn't aware that Miranda was your aunt,' Rachel said with a puzzled look.

'Well, she isn't really. Not technically mind you, but in all respects, she's been rather a guiding force in my upbringing.'

At that moment Miranda walked in and added, 'A good one, I hope.' Turning to Rachel she explained. 'Adam's parents, the Brabazons are dear friends and are practically family, considering that we've lived under the same roof at the Mission in Nairobi for over two decades.'

'Yes and I've called her Aunt Miranda ever since I was a babe-in-arms. She has been a part of the Mission and the family for as long back as I can remember.'

'That is very interesting. Are you back for good now, Miranda?' Rachel asked as Miranda helped herself to some kedgeree.

'Good heavens, certainly not! My home is in Kenya now. Can't imagine living anywhere else. But I have had quite enough of Mission work and there are new people coming out all the time to help with the Mission. I feel quite redundant amidst the sea of fresh young faces. Hence the vacation.'

Adam added, 'Well deserved, I should think. But don't get too comfortable. I've got a good mind to rope you in for the safari work, once we get back. God knows, I'll need all the help I can get.'

Miranda shook her head. 'I shan't be any good as one of the guns, I'm afraid.'

'What rot! You are one of the best shots I've ever come across!' Adam retorted.

Miranda smiled and said, 'You seem to be forgetting that I'm not at an age where I have any inclination to go traipsing all over the Mara anymore. I want a bit of peace and quiet now.'

Adam responded with affection, 'Well alright then, you can see to the town work. There'll be tons of correspondence once we get started. I am hopeless with mail and of course I won't have the time when I'm on the Mara.'

Rachel interjected at this point, 'At the risk of sounding terribly ignorant, what exactly is the Mara?'

Miranda answered, 'The term originates from the tribe Maasai Mara. The land originally belonged to them but now we locals refer to the large and extensive land and the game on it, as the Mara. It is one of the most amazing places on the planet, if one is interested in spotting game. It is home to a huge population of lions, cheetahs and elephants, and is quite famous for the "Great Migration" – an annual migration of zebra, gazelle and wildebeest to and from the Serengeti every year through July to October.'

Rachel said, 'It all sounds rather exciting.'

Adam didn't look the least bit excited as he responded with a glum face. 'I'd like to invite you over to experience it first hand, but as things stand I'm not quite sure when we can start. There is a little matter of stuck finances. Not to put too fine a point on it, Lord Marbury had promised to help me with finance for the operations but now...' he paused.

Jeremy spoke, 'Ah! I see.'

Adam looked at him speculatively and said, 'And I'm sure you will also see *why* I'd be very interested in helping you both get to the bottom of this as quickly as you can.'

'Glad to hear it. You could start by telling us whatever you can recollect about the events that led up to the shooting on the fateful day,' was Jeremy's response.

'Certainly. Let's resume our walk after breakfast and I'll fill you both in,' Adam said as he helped himself to some eggs and toast.

III

The walk took them down the meandering pathways of the estate that led towards the hills. The sky was overcast in places and the golden sunbeams continued to play hide and seek with the landscape. Rachel was thankful that she was warmly clad as a cold wind whipped about them. They were walking through a grove of elm and birch. Snow had been predicted in a day or two but for now the trees swept up their stark arms towards the sky and the ground was hard despite a carpet of dried leaves which crunched underfoot. She imagined that a dusting of snow for a day or two would turn the entire horizon into a winter wonderland.

As if in tune with her thoughts Adam shivered. 'Brr...not used to the freezing cold. Give me the blazing sun of Africa any day. I don't know how you people stand this English weather.'

'One gets used to it, I suppose but then you haven't been here long enough for that. For those of us who have, I'll admit that we do get gloomy about the cold from time to time. After all, it is a national pastime to grumble about the weather but here's a secret most people don't know – somewhere deep down we also surreptitiously enjoy our winters. The brisk walks, crackling log fires and then the beauty of the first snow, the slanting sunlight. I mean, look around you. You must admit this light and colour play is heavenly. Almost makes one overlook the nip in the air.'

Adam shook his head, 'Nip in the air? It's alright for you lot to think of this arctic weather as a nip in the air. I can tell you, if I have to spend another month here, I'll probably freeze to death or become suicidal, whichever comes first!'

Rachel laughed.

Adam continued, 'Which reminds me, the sooner you get to the bottom of this nasty shooting business, the sooner I can pack my bags and head home.'

Rachel nodded, 'Your observations on the day of the shooting would be a good place to start.'

'Hmm, let me see; the events of the day, well, we started pretty early and we were all riding in a group with the hounds. Once we entered the woods, some of the riders dispersed away from the track to take the more adventurous route through the woods. I was one of them. I was accompanied by Roddy and his father, Baron Braybourne – he's a sporting old chap and quite the equestrian. Apparently he's been shooting up at Marbury ever since he was a lad when the previous Earl was alive, so he knows his way around these woods like the back of his hand. The course he chose was quite difficult and we jumped over quite a few fallen logs, streams and so forth. But somewhere along the way, I stopped to take a breather and got down from my horse to stretch my legs and have a cigarette and by the time I was done, the others were out of sight. That's when I heard the gunshot coming from somewhere up on the hill to my right.'

Jeremy spoke, 'The Chief Inspector informed us that you were the first to arrive at the scene of the shooting.'

'Yes. There was a path that went up the hill about five hundred yards to my right. See that spot over there? That's where I was when I heard the shot. And look on the other side, over there – that is where the path goes up.'

Jeremy nodded. 'Right. Now I want you to think back carefully and tell me exactly what you did after that.'

'I mounted my horse and made my way up the hill. But from this end of the woods, it's quite a steep climb and half way up it gets very narrow. And as I didn't fancy going horseback, up a narrow, steep, unknown terrain, I dismounted and tethered my horse to a tree half way through and hiked up on foot rest of the way.'

'Did you see anyone or anything while you were making the climb?' Rachel asked.

'Well, yes and no. I saw no one and heard nothing but the call of alarmed birds and creatures but then...I heard a twig snap somewhere close by. Now I know you're going to think that there could be a hundred reasons for a twig snapping in the woods, but I did get a distinct impression that someone was watching me. In fact I'm sure someone was. I have a sixth sense about these things and I learnt a thing or two about tracking back in Africa and it seemed to me that whoever it was, was taking great pains to conceal themselves from me. I did look about but unfortunately I could not spot anyone.

And once I reached the clearing and saw Lord Marbury sprawled up there bleeding to death, I couldn't care less if I was being watched. I ran up to him and felt for a pulse and found that he was still breathing and then I started hollering for help.'

Rachel asked, 'But what about the Lordship's horse, Painter? We were told that he galloped downhill and alerted others to the incident. Did you not encounter him on your way up?'

'Goodness, no! The track I took up was so narrow that if the horse had decided to take it he would've most certainly mowed me down in the process. You see, there are three different paths that lead up to the clearing – one from the house towards the south and two from the woods. Lucky for me, Lord Marbury's horse was sensible enough to take the wider path down which reaches the woods towards the north. Apparently that was where most of the hunting party was when they spotted Painter galloping down rider-less.'

Jeremy spoke. 'That is very interesting. Can you lead the way? I think it is important for us to take a good look at the clearing and see it for ourselves. I'm quite certain that the police have literally left no stone unturned in their investigation but it may help us to get an added perspective.'

Adam responded, 'Certainly! The police did categorically tell us that the area was off limits for a while longer but I don't suppose the Chief Inspector will make a fuss if you two visit.'

As they trudged up, Jeremy asked, 'Can you recollect anything strange from the days leading up to the shooting, any untoward incident or conversation?'

'Well, there was this incident at the village pub some time ago, although I don't really know if I should tell you about it or if it has any bearing on the case at all.'

'What was it?' Rachel asked.

'I had just stopped for a pint of bitter at the pub when I saw a pair of toughs roughing Neville up. And they looked as though they meant business. Poor chap was pinned against the bar, looking dreadfully pale and I don't know what would have ensued had I not intervened and put the fear of God in them.'

'Lucky for him you were there then. When was this?' Jeremy queried.

'I can't remember exactly but I'd say roughly about two weeks ago.'

'Do you know who they were?' Rachel asked.

'Well, no. It wasn't exactly a social interaction and I didn't have the pleasure of being formally introduced while I was landing punches.'

Rachel chuckled.

Adam continued, 'And Neville, being the tight-lipped arse that he is, pardon my French, didn't volunteer any further information on our walk back to the Hall. Perhaps you could ask him. All I know is that I hadn't seen them around these parts before. But here's the strange bit – he mumbled something about being knee deep in debt but that he had an idea that all his troubles would be over soon. In the wake of the shooting one can't help wondering what this idea was,' Adam concluded with a sideways glance at Jeremy.

'Hmm...interesting observation.' Jeremy said slowly.

Rachel asked Adam bluntly, 'Do you think Neville shot his uncle?'

Adam shook his head, 'No, I don't. And he seems to have a pretty good alibi for the time of the shooting. Besides, he's a terrible shot. But one can't overlook the possibility that he got someone else to do his dirty work for him. Where this kind of wealth is involved, we have a saying back in Kenya – anything goes.'

'Hmm. Any ideas on who this accomplice may have been?'

'If I were you, I'd interrogate the chaps who roughed him up. Looks as though Neville's gain would benefit them as well. Also, I saw him a day or two before the shooting, talking to some chap in the woods. I wouldn't have paid much attention but for the fact that Neville had a rather shifty look about him. I didn't get a good look at the other fellow. He walked away as I approached but I got the impression that I had seen him before. Probably an employee here. Could have been the gamekeeper but I can't be sure.'

'I think we had better have a word with Neville – the sooner the better,' Jeremy said as Rachel nodded her head in agreement.

They walked up the rest of the way in silence, lost in thought.

As they reached the clearing, Adam said in a hushed voice, 'That's strange. There seems to be somebody there. Probably another sensation hunter. They've been crawling all over the place ever since the shooting.'

They could all see the back of a man in a large black coat and hat. He appeared to be bending down and peering at the ground near a clump of bushes.

Adam shouted as he took long strides towards the man, 'I say, Sir, whoever you are, you are trespassing. This is private property and a crime scene.'

The man's back seemed to stiffen and then he slowly straightened up and turned around to face them calmly. Rachel noticed he was elderly without the frailty one expects in the elderly. Up close he was about sixty-five, had white hair and there was an aura of power about him. The kind of personal power that one sees in very successful and often extremely wealthy men. She took in his broad build, deep brown eyes and handsome features and instinctively knew who he was, even before Adam sheepishly greeted him and made introductions.

Baron Braybourne had returned to Marbury Hall.

Chapter Six

By late afternoon the sky had darkened and the first fat snowflakes had started a leisurely descent from the wintry sky. Snow had been expected but the sudden drop in temperature by half a dozen degrees had not. Despite several fires blazing away in various rooms, Rachel felt the large house was comparable to an icebox. After a heavy luncheon, Rachel and Jeremy were ensconced in the oak panelled library with Baron Braybourne at his request. The log fire was crackling and they each had a snifter of brandy for added warmth. The lamps had been lit.

The Baron sank back into his armchair and took his time to light his pipe. His gaze was fixed on the window with a view of the woods and looming dark hills silhouetted in the distance. He puffed a plume of blue smoke out and spoke in his rich baritone voice. 'I've asked you both here for this interview because I think it's time to make a clean breast of things. You see, Magnus was worried about something in the days leading up to the shooting. I've known him long enough to know that it was something quite out of the ordinary. So on the night before the incident I managed to corner him and ask him what it was. He said he was not ready to tell me yet but...'

As Rachel and Jeremy remained silent, he brought his gaze back to them and continued, 'He asked me cryptic questions regarding the estate's entail and if he could fight it. If he could prove and legitimise a male heir.'

'But he has daughters,' Rachel said in a reflective tone.

The Baron nodded and spoke slowly, 'Exactly what I told him. I said, my dear boy, you can't just whip out a son from nowhere, like a rabbit out of a magician's hat and expect everyone to accept him as your heir.'

'What was his response?' Rachel asked.

'Well, he told me that he had no doubt about the boy's paternity and would try his darndest to prove his son's right to be heir apparent as opposed to that incompetent fool, Neville. And I told him that Neville may be a fool but that it was a great mistake to underestimate the power of sheer ambition or for that matter, to assume that Neville would just politely step aside and bid adieu to a great fortune such as this. And all because he had suddenly decided Neville was not suitable and had a more likely candidate in mind.'

Jeremy spoke, 'Did he say who he had in mind?'

'No. He was too crafty for that. Dodged all my questions with effortless ease. But after a great deal of going back and forth, he did tell me that a long time ago, before he married Catherine and before he came into this title or made my acquaintance, he was involved with another young lady and their union ended unhappily within a few months.'

'Was he married to this lady?' Jeremy asked.

The Baron shook his head. '*That* you see, is the trouble. I do not know. He may have been. He simply said that the lady in question disappeared from his life only to resurface recently with the claim that she had borne him a son. In or out of wedlock being the moot question here.'

'Goodness! Does the Countess know?' Rachel asked.

'I don't think so. He did tell me that I was the only person other than the lady concerned and thereby her son, I presume, who knew about this. Considering he was shot the very next morning, I don't know if he even had the chance to confide in Catherine.'

Rachel was thoughtful. 'Well, if he had been married and didn't divorce his first wife legally, it would complicate things considerably for the Countess after all these years.'

The Baron nodded. 'Quite. And unless there is a birth certificate to prove otherwise, there is also the small matter of the law of this land that does not recognise illegitimate offspring and thereby prevents them from being the heir apparent to such a title. A fact that I duly brought to his notice.'

'What was Lord Marbury's response?' Jeremy asked.

'He told me quite emphatically that the boy was his and that he would discuss it further in the fullness of time. For the moment he planned to discuss it with his friend and confidante, Winston, the following week.'

Rachel spoke. 'Are you referring to Mr. Churchill?'

'The same. They were supposed to meet a week later at the Astor's house party at Cliveden. I reckon Magnus wanted to know the social and political implications if he were to change his will and engage the top solicitors in the land to fight for his son's right to ascension.'

'Would that be possible?' Jeremy queried.

The Baron smiled, 'Well, if a team of legal experts were to find a loop hole in this estate's entail, which would allow him to change his will, I should think that there was a chance of bringing it about. You see, back in 1925 the fee tail or entail was abolished but when Magnus inherited, he did so as the heir presumptive. And while there is a clause which enables the heir apparent to disentail, technically Magnus may not have the authority to do so but his first born son, if proven legitimate, would be considered as the heir apparent. It is a tricky business and Magnus would of course be making history if he were to succeed. But then he was, oh I am sorry, *is* that sort of man. Once he makes up his mind to do something, it's as good as done.'

Jeremy asked, 'Can you be quite certain that apart from the lady in question and yourself, no one else knew about his intention to change his will and subsequently the fortunes of several people involved?'

'I am sorry. I don't really know. I suppose he may have discussed it with his son but since Magnus and I had no further conversations regarding this matter, I can only surmise and hope that he kept a secret of such magnitude to himself.'

'Lord Braybourne, did you inform the police about this conversation?' Jeremy asked.

'I'm ashamed to say that I did not, as I foolishly thought at the time that it was an intensely private matter and had Magnus succumbed to his injuries, publicising his intentions to change his will would have only caused pain to the existing beneficiaries. I felt there was no need for indiscretion on my part and that it had no bearing on this case but now in retrospect, I fear I may have been wrong.'

Jeremy nodded. 'I'm afraid I have to agree with you there. We must inform Chief Inspector Harrow about this. All things considered, it may have been the primary motive for his attempted murder.'

'Well, Mr. Richards, I can only hope that this will help and not add to the prevailing confusion; muddy the waters further, if you get my drift. After all, there is an off-chance that it had nothing whatsoever to do with the shooting.'

Jeremy shrugged. 'Yes, on the other hand, we cannot disregard the fact that it may have everything to do with it. One last question, as one of Lord Marbury's oldest friends, you must have some suspicion as to who this lady might be.'

'Well, I think I can guess but I should not like to say as I can't be certain. You must understand that it would be mere speculation on my part.'

Rachel spoke. 'But surely, you must realise how important it is for us to know your thoughts around this, even if you can't be certain...'

The Baron contemplated her words in silence and then sighed. 'Well, in for a penny, in for a pound, I suppose. The only person I know who has come back into his life after a good many years is Ada Cellini and before you ask, yes she does have a son from a former marriage, long before she achieved her current level of fame and success. Her son's name is Andrew Clayton and he's about the right age too, around twenty three or twenty four. I've known him ever since he was a boy. He was at Eton and then Oxford with my son, Roderick.'

Jeremy spoke, 'Who does he get his last name – Clayton from?'

The Baron said, 'Why, from Donald Clayton, purportedly Andrew's father.'

Rachel said slowly, 'Donald Clayton – the name sounds familiar.'

'I wouldn't be surprised. He is considered to be some sort of a king maker in his field. He has been known to make or break careers in theatrical circles. He also happens to be Ada's third husband and the man who gave her son his last name. Well, that is, apart from being her financial manager. If Ada is to be believed, the latter function is the primary role he plays in her life,' the Baron said with a twinkle in his eye.

Rachel smiled. 'I see. We will have to have a word with Madame Cellini about all of this. It goes without saying that we'll go about it as discreetly as we can. But is there any way we can get in touch with either Donald or Andrew Clayton?'

The Baron shrugged, 'Well, I don't know about Donald. Rumour has it that he's been lying low somewhere on the continent since September, ever since that nasty business involving him and that queer actor was plastered all over the tabloids.'

Rachel spoke in a puzzled tone, 'I'm sorry but I think we missed that bit of news, we must have been on our way to India at the time.'

The Baron chuckled. 'You didn't miss much. Just that some nosy reporter found and printed some compromising pictures of the two men. It did create quite a scandal but if you ask me it didn't come as much of a surprise, as Donald was always known in his circle to be er...batting for the wrong side, so to speak.'

Rachel grinned. 'I see. That makes things a bit clearer. What about Ada's son, Andrew Clayton? It would aid our investigation to know if Lord Marbury had spoken with him, regarding his intention to name him as his heir. I know this may sound like an imposition, Lord Braybourne but would it be at all possible for you to arrange a meeting with him?'

'That should be easy. Ada asked me if I could give her son a lift from London this morning and I did. Andrew is here at Marbury Hall as we speak.'

Rachel said, 'Oh? I didn't see him at lunch.'

'Yes, well the boys – Roderick and Andrew took my car into the village for some repairs. They must have lunched at Marbury Arms.'

Rachel smiled, 'Thank you Lord Braybourne. You have been most helpful.'

'Please don't mention it. I am glad to have gotten it off my chest. If there is anything else I can help you with please don't hesitate to ask. I wish you both luck and hope you bring the person who did this to justice.'

Chapter Seven

'So, what do you think, Jeremy?' Rachel asked him as they headed back to their room through the winding staircases and corridors.

'About what?'

'About the weather...' Rachel responded with good humoured sarcasm.

Jeremy smiled and took the bait. 'I think we could get very comfortable if they've lit the fire in your room. We've got a good three hours before the dinner gong goes off.'

She rolled her eyes, 'Jeremy! About what the Baron had to say. As far as I can see, I think this has opened a whole new can of worms. Don't you?'

'Hmm, worms. I do hope you'll keep this conversation in mind the next time you complain about my shortcomings in the romance department.'

Rachel laughed, 'Just for that I think I'll call your bluff, Mister. Brr...also it is rather cold. I don't mind snuggling up in front of the fire at all.'

'Perennially at your service, Madame,' Jeremy said with a smile and a playful bow as he held the door open for her.

As they laughed and entered, the maid looked up from the fireplace and apologised. 'I'm sorry, madam. I was just getting the fire going again and I've turned down the bed. I'll come back later to help you dress for dinner.'

'That will be fine, thank you Summer. Oh, I almost forgot. I think I've got a spot of grease on my blue silk. Do you think you can get it off in time for dinner? I daresay, I packed in a hurry and overlooked it.'

'I'll see to it madam. Tea will be served in the sitting room in half an hour,' she said as she took out the dress from the wardrobe.

'I think I'll skip tea today, thanks. I am rather cold and tired. I've a good mind to take a nap for an hour or so.'

'Right madam, if you need anything else, please ring for me.'

'Just the dress, thanks. I'll expect you back at six thirty then.'

As the maid nodded and left carrying the dress out, Jeremy smiled and said, 'I thought she was never going to leave. Pity she's made the bed. All that hard work for nothing.'

Rachel giggled as he locked the door and took her in his arms.

II

It was nearly seven in the evening when Rachel rang for the maid. Ten minutes later, the door opened and instead of Summer, a new maid entered.

Rachel asked, 'Where is Summer?'

'Sorry madam, Summer is now't to be found, so Mrs. Simmons – the housekeeper sent me to help you in her place.'

'But she's got my dress! She was going to remove a spot of grease from it. Can you please go and check if she's left it in the laundry or the ironing room and retrieve it? It's a blue silk and has a Schiaparelli label. By the way, what's your name?'

'It's Ivy, madam.'

'Well then Ivy, I'm relying on you. Now please hurry, I'm already late,' she told the girl with a smile, as she adjusted the belt on her kimono dressing gown.

'Yes, right away, madam.'

Ten minutes later, as Rachel finished applying the last touches of make-up and removed the curlers from her hair, there was another discreet knock on her door before Ivy came back in looking ashen faced. She was carrying a crumpled blue dress in her arms.

'I am so sorry, madam. I did find your dress lying under one of the ironing tables but 'tis in a right state, it is!'

Rachel sighed and thanked her years of good breeding. It certainly helped in keeping her calm as she examined the beleaguered state of one of her favourite dresses. 'Oh well, I suppose I will have to make do with something less formal then. Wait a minute! What are all these brownish marks on it? It's still damp. Ivy, did you spill something on it?'

'No madam, I brought it just the way I found it. I am terribly sorry.'

Rachel took a closer look at the marks, brought the dress up to her nose and sniffed, 'Oh my God! This is blood. Quick girl, show me the way to your ironing room. Something isn't right.'

'I am not sure Mrs. Simmons will approve, madam...'

'Never mind your Mrs. Simmons. I promise I'll deal with her and make sure you don't get into any trouble over this, alright? Now, lead the way please. Hurry.'

As the two women made their way through the corridors, past the green baize door and into the staff area, they got puzzled looks from bewildered footmen, kitchen maids, valets and various household staff till they reached a painted white door, which Ivy opened for her. It was a midsized room equipped with three ironing tables and had a glass paned door leading to another room.

Rachel looked around and said, 'There are three tables and only two irons here. Where's the third iron?'

Ivy looked about her nervously as she answered, 'I'm sure I don't know, madam. We shouldn't be here, really. I could get the sack for this.'

Rachel walked towards the connecting door with glass panes. She opened it and walked into what looked like a large linen room. There were about a dozen shelves stacked with neatly folded bed sheets and bath towels.

On her left she spotted an enormous laundry hamper, presumably where the soiled linen was dumped. She walked up to it and lifted the lid. Moving the topmost bundles of sheets and towels, she gasped.

At that moment, a tall stately woman in a black dress and stiff lace collar entered the ironing room and spoke in a cold, authoritative voice, 'Ivy, what is going on?'

Ivy shrugged helplessly and motioned towards the linen room.

The housekeeper walked through the door and spotting Rachel by the laundry basket, she asked politely, 'May I help you, madam? I am Mrs. Simmons, the housekeeper.'

Rachel looked at her and said calmly, 'Yes, Mrs. Simmons, you may. Kindly lock up this room and telephone the police. One of your maids has just been murdered.'

III

Half an hour later, Rachel had just finished giving her statement to the police in the sitting room. As she left it, she almost bumped into the Countess.

The Countess spoke. 'Dear me! I am sorry, Rachel. I just heard. What a terrible ordeal it must have been for you, finding that girl's body. It doesn't bear thinking.'

'Not as bad as it must have been for that poor girl – Summer. I believe she was your gamekeeper's daughter.'

The Countess answered in her vague way, 'Yes. Oh, I do hope someone has informed him about this. What a ghastly thing to have happened. Do you have any idea as to how she was killed?'

'I can't be sure, Lady Marbury, but by the look of it she seems to have been clobbered to death with a heavy coal iron. I found it in the hamper next to the body.'

'How awful! Come and join us in the library. We've all gathered there since the police have taken over the sitting room. Mrs. Meade, our cook has sent up some sandwiches and cold cuts. We cancelled dinner of course. Seemed the right thing to do under the circumstances.'

'I agree, Countess. But I hope you won't mind terribly if I don't join the others in the library. I'd rather go straight up to my room. I am feeling positively knackered.'

'How thoughtless of me. Of course you must do that. I'm sure I wouldn't want to face a lot of people after an ordeal like that. I'll have Mrs. Meade send a tray up to you.'

'That is very kind of you, Countess. Also...I was wondering if I could make a telephone call to my mother at Rutherford Hall.'

'Why, certainly. You could use the extension in the morning room. It offers more privacy than the one in the hall.'

'Thank you. I shall.'

'I think I'll inform your husband that you are going up. It's best not to be alone at a time like this,' she said, as she moved away to issue instructions to the butler, who was hovering in the hall.

Five minutes later, Rachel was on the telephone with her mother, Lady Elizabeth at Rutherford Hall.

'Darling Mums, I need your help. I was wondering if I could steal one of your housemaids for a bit...Yes? Oh, good! I need someone with spunk so I was thinking of Betsy, if you could spare her for a week or so...Lovely! That'll be perfect. Now here's what I want her to do...'

Chapter Eight

An hour later, Jeremy was in the Butler's pantry with the Police Sergeant and Constable questioning the servants. So far they had very little to go on. They had just finished questioning the family and guests upstairs. There were different accounts of who was seen near or inside the linen room between 4.30 and 7.15. Out of the nine housemaids, two kitchen maids, three footmen, four valets and three lady's maids, no one recalled having seen Summer in the linen or the ironing room even though several valets and lady's maids had used both. No one had bothered to check why the third iron was missing except for Lady Claire's maid, Myrtle.

She informed them, 'I did wonder. Both the irons were occupied and I had to wait till Tilly – that is Her Ladyship's maid and Lord Braybourne's valet had finished. I noticed the third one was missing but I just thought the boot boy had taken it out the back way to coal it. That is part of his duties and we all know that he is shoddy about getting the irons ready in time before the dressing gong goes. We've complained about it to Mrs. Simmons and Mr. Hobbs often enough!'

Billy, the scrawny young boot boy was duly interrogated and pooh-poohed any suggestion regarding shoddiness on his part. He informed them that all the irons had been coaled and left in the ironing room by 4.15 and no, he did not recall seeing Summer but he had seen Mr. Pelham enter the servant's passage as Billy himself had gone out the back way for a well deserved smoke. He had not thought it odd as a lot of the house party used the back entrance owing to the fact that it was a shortcut to the garage.

The chauffeur and the footmen were interviewed next. They had nothing much to contribute except that they had seen Mr. Roderick Cartwright and Mr. Andrew Clayton return from the village at about five. The men had brought the car to the garage and handed the car over to the chauffeur. While the chauffeur was parking the car, he had seen them take the back entrance to the house. Post which, Lord Braybourne had come out through the passage to inspect his car. The footmen corroborated the chauffeur's story and said that they had seen all three men come through the servant's hall and informed the police that they had taken the servant's passage.

Jeremy made a mental note to question both the boys and the Baron later in case they had heard or seen anything out of the ordinary, or if they had passed anyone coming from the other direction. There was the chilling possibility that they passed by the ironing room door within minutes of the murder.

Tilly – the Countess' maid was called in next. She was tearful and looked haggard as she informed them that she had caught two housemaids idling about in the ironing room when she had entered and had packed them off with a flea in their ear for shirking work. 'I had no idea that the poor girl was lying dead in the next room, sir! Oh, the poor child!'

As she burst into another round of sniffling, Jeremy proffered his handkerchief and offered her a glass of water. After she had a sip, he changed the subject to get her mind off the dead girl. He asked, 'How is it that you are addressed by your first name? I thought it was customary for a lady's maid in a household like this to be addressed by her last name.'

Tilly dabbed her eyes with the handkerchief Jeremy had supplied and spoke, 'Yes, sir that is true but owing to my last name also being Simmons, like the housekeeper's, Mr. Hobbs thought it would create less confusion in the servant's hall. Besides, I've always been Tilly to her ladyship ever since I joined service as a girl, sir.'

The two young housemaids who were allegedly idling about in the ironing room were interrogated next. They were sisters – Nora and Mary Jones and had been recruited by Mrs. Simmons merely a month ago from the neighbouring village of Snodsbury. Both were nervous wrecks as they entered the room and Jeremy tried to calm them down long enough to get some information but in vain. Nora, the younger of the two told him in her round eyed way that they were sure the ghost that haunted the servant's quarters had finally got his revenge.

Jeremy sighed and asked, 'What do you mean the ghost got his revenge? What ghost?'

The older one answered, 'Surely you've heard, sir? Why, it's the fifth Earl's spirit that walks in the dead of the night. When we go upstairs to bed, we have to knock on the door to the women's passage and ask for permission to enter. He gets you otherwise. Everyone knows that!'

While Jeremy smiled inwardly and wondered why on earth the fifth Earl would spend his ghostly time parading about in the servant's sleeping quarters, he couldn't help asking, 'Why would you think he took revenge between 4.30 and 7.15 in the evening? Surely that isn't as per his proper haunting schedule which according to you, seems to be the dead of the night?'

'Well, sir, can't say why. All I know is that girl – Summer, never listened to the others and she used to laugh about him. Said she didn't believe in no ghosts. She never knocked to ask for his permission either and she once told us that she'd blow him a kiss if she ever saw him. That's what's done her in, I say, mocking his spirit. Ghosts don't like that.'

'I see. And have you ever seen or heard this ghost?'

'Why, yes sir! Well, to be honest, we ain't ever seen him, but Nora and I share the first room on the landing and we can hear him walking about outside our door. A few nights ago we got so scared that we stuck a chair under the door knob, didn't we Nora?'

'Aye, sir, we did done that,' was Nora's wide eyed response accompanied by a vigorous nodding of the head.

Jeremy thought of informing them that as per lore, ghosts could walk through walls and would obviously not be hampered by doors or chairs but then Mrs. Simmons would probably not thank him for scaring two of her newest recruits to death, so he simply asked, 'How do you know it was the ghost? Surely, it could have been another servant you heard.'

'Why, no sir. He wears boots, you see and men aren't allowed in the women's sleeping quarters. Mrs. Simmons makes it a point to lock up before turning in for the night.'

Jeremy made a mental note to ask Mrs. Simmons about the keys to that door. He smiled and thanked them for their valuable inputs and said, 'One last question. What time do you normally hear this ghost walking about?'

Mary answered in all seriousness, 'Why, sir! In the dead of the night!'

Chapter Nine

Meanwhile back in her room, Rachel sat at her study table as strains of a piano forte wafted up to her ears from somewhere in the house. Her mind was in a whirl. She and Jeremy had been here for a total of forty eight hours and the murderer had struck for a second time, this time with greater success and right under their noses. Why kill a housemaid? And why Summer particularly? What had the girl known that she was attacked and killed in such a brutal way? Rachel knew it could have been done to possibly silence her or perhaps the girl had seen or heard something that she wasn't supposed to.

She wanted to know more about the girl but she knew instinctively that she wouldn't get very far if she went about questioning the servants on her own. It was simply not done in a household of this sort, if her short trip to the linen room was anything to go by. There was a distinct separation between the upstairs and downstairs, and the set protocol frowned upon anyone from upstairs, especially for a house guest to be seen in the servant's hall, let alone getting into cosy chats with them.

It was different for Jeremy who was invited to be part of the investigative team by the Police Sergeant but she would have to have patience and wait for Betsy's arrival. Like Chief Inspector Harrow, she too needed a mole on the inside, someone who could get information from the staff without arousing too much suspicion downstairs.

Then there was the question of Neville Pelham. Everything pointed to him, but far too obviously for her liking. He may not be the sharpest knife in the drawer but he was no village idiot either, of that she was sure. After all, he did have a watertight alibi for the time of the Earl's shooting. He was vouched for by the butler and two other house guests. They had given the police statements that they had seen him partaking breakfast in the dining hall when the shot rang out. Adam Brabazon had suggested an accomplice. She also wondered if Neville had any inkling about Lord Marbury's intentions to disinherit him. Lady Claire was a suspect too. Daughter or not, being betrothed to Neville, she stood as much to lose as he did, if the Earl survived to change his will.

Then there was the Countess' sister, Miranda. Did she have any role in all of this? Despite outward appearances, could she and the Countess have some rivalry which went beyond the mere sibling variety? What about Ada Cellini and her son Roderick? It was possible that the soprano may not have been the Earl's ex-wife, the Baron himself had admitted that he was not certain. What if she was simply one of his disgruntled ex-lovers and she had killed him for some travesty in the past. But on the other hand if she was the mother of the Earl's son, both mother and son would only stand to lose by Lord Marbury's untimely demise.

As her thoughts flew fast and furious, she did something she had never found necessary to do before, in the past four cases that she had solved. She took a sheet of writing paper from the desk in her room and started making a list of suspects.

Before long there was a knock on her door and Ivy came in carrying a tray of sandwiches. She placed the tray on the coffee table and hovered, folding and unfolding her hands.

Rachel looked at her quizzically, 'Thank you, Ivy. Is there anything else?'

'Well, madam. I heard from Mr. Hobbs that your husband is with the police.'

'In a manner of speaking, yes he is. But never mind that, I can see there is something on your mind.'

'Yes madam. You see, he and the police were asking us questions about our whereabouts and such in Mr. Hobbs's pantry. I just finished telling them that I had seen and heard nothing but...'

'But what?'

'But that isn't entirely true, madam. I didn't want to say all I knew in front of all those men. Now, I shouldn't like to speak ill of the dead but Summer was the bad kind, the kind that makes the rest of us housemaids look bad, if you know what I mean.'

'I'm afraid I don't. What exactly do you mean by bad, Ivy?'

'Now the rest of us know our place, madam and Mrs. Simmons is awful strict about the likes of us mixin' with the house guests.'

'Yes?'

'I don't know how to tell you this madam but she never followed rules, and she was always tardy but that isn't what I'm trying to say...'

'Let me guess. She did something that was not right for someone in her position to do...perhaps with one of the houseguests?'

Ivy gave a sigh of relief and said, 'Yes, Madam. She had something going on with Mr. Pelham. At least Billy, that's the boot boy, he said he saw em kissing before they went in to the gamekeeper's cottage in the woods. He told us that Mr. Pelham was havin' a bit of fun on the side. I didn't quite know how to tell the police that but after she was killed, I thought I ought to tell someone. What if it had something to do with her gettin' killed like that?'

'You did the right thing by telling me but why did Billy not relay that information to Mr. Hobbs or Mrs. Simmons himself?'

'He's right scared of them. We all are. They've always been nice enough to us but...'

'I see. Right. Now, I want you to think carefully and tell me if anyone else was around when Billy told you about what he had seen.'

'Yes. He came running into the servant's hall, all out of breath and I remember James – the footman and Tilly were there too – that's the Ladyship's maid.'

'If that be the case, I'm surprised it didn't become common knowledge sooner.'

'It was Tilly, madam. She put the fear of God in all of us. She boxed Billy in the ears and told him to stop talking filth and spreading lies. She also told James and me that if we spoke about it to another living soul, she'd speak to her Ladyship and have us sacked. Seeing as Mr. Pelham is engaged to Lady Claire, it didn't surprise me. Tilly is like that. She'd kill to avoid scandal or dishonour upon her Ladyship's family. Oh! I didn't mean...about Tilly...I mean...'

'Don't worry. I know what you mean. It's alright. You can relax, Ivy. No one is going to arrest Tilly for being loyal to her mistress. Now, is there anything else that you would like to tell me?'

Ivy seemed hesitant as though she wanted to speak further but then changing her mind in the end, she said, 'If you don't mind, madam, I had better be going back to the servant's hall now or Mrs. Simmons will have my hide for sure. We're shorthanded as it is, what with Summer gone and all...'

Rachel nodded, and as Ivy reached the door, she said, 'Ivy, if there is anything else you wish to share, anything at all, please don't hesitate to tell me. There is a murderer on the loose so I'd advise you to be careful and if you see or hear anything odd do come and tell me as soon as you can.'

'Yes, madam.' Then as she turned the doorknob, she glanced back at Rachel with a nervous look and said, 'I hope I shan't get into any trouble for this.'

'I'll make sure that you don't. You can trust me on that.'

Chapter Ten

The next morning, Jeremy came into the room with a pleased look upon his face and greeted her with a cheerful good morning kiss.

Rachel said groggily, 'It's a bit early in the day to look this pleased. Whatever you've been up to, darling, I'm quite certain there's a law against it.'

'On the contrary, my love, I am happy to announce that the harness of secrecy and discretion has finally been lifted from our heads. In the wake of yesterday's murder, I have permission from the Countess herself to take over Lord Marbury's study and conduct our investigation in full swing.'

Rachel lifted herself on to an elbow and answered with a smile, 'That is good news. I was getting a bit tired of masquerading about as a house guest with an open secret.'

'And we have a meeting with the estate's executor, Mr. Phipps in half an hour, so chop, chop. I'd like you to join me in the study for that.'

'I'm sure you would. Well, I had better be up and about then. No rest for the wicked as they say.'

Jeremy grinned back, 'Quite right too. After meeting Mr. Phipps, I think we ought to have a tête-à-tête with Ada Cellini and her son. What do you think?'

'Sounds like a plan, darling. Oh, and while you're at it, please schedule a hammer and tongs session with Neville Pelham as well. I have recently been made privy to some rather interesting information regarding the gent.'

Jeremy raised an eyebrow, 'What? There's more?'

'Wait till you hear this...'

Rachel told him about her conversation with Ivy the night before and he let out a low whistle. 'Do the man's shenanigans ever end?'

Rachel responded, 'I just hope that given his reputation or the lamentable lack of it, we don't have to add murder on that glowing list.'

II

'Ah, Mr. Phipps. Glad you could make it at such short notice. I am Jeremy Richards and this is my wife, Rachel.'

'Yes, I met Lady Marbury just now and she told me that you were expecting me. She also gave me to believe that you were private detectives,' Mr. Phipps said with a raised eyebrow and a hint of a smile. He was in his fifties, dressed in an expensive navy pin stripe suit. He had a round face, thinning hair and friendly brown eyes.

'Indeed.'

'And although she did not elaborate further, I am at a loss as to how I may be of help to you.'

'Well, Mr. Phipps, as you know that the household is in the midst of a murder investigation and certain things have come to light in the past few days and I'll come straight to the point. We would very much like to know if Lord Marbury had been in touch with you regarding the estate's entail in the recent past.'

'Hardly likely, he's in a coma, or haven't you detected that yet,' Mr. Phipps asked with a twinkle in his eye.

Jeremy responded with an amused look, 'Yes, we are aware of that. Let me rephrase that. Did he get in touch with you before the unfortunate incident to arrange a meeting, regarding the estate's entail?'

'Funny you should mention it but we did have a meeting lined up on the twenty eighth, which obviously did not take place owing to the fact that someone shot him two days prior to that. But I'm afraid I can't be sure about what he wanted to discuss. All I know is that he insisted on coming up to my offices in London. I did think it odd at the time.'

'Why would you think it odd?' Rachel asked.

'I suppose because in the past it was customary for me to come down to Marbury Hall if he needed to look at deeds or estate investments, papers and so forth. That's how we've done it for years. Why do you ask?'

Jeremy spoke, 'As the estate's executor, you would have a pretty good estimate about the entail. Would you say it was water tight or did it have enough flexibility to offer a change in his will?'

'Well, this is rather unorthodox. His Lordship is not dead yet. I do not think I am at liberty to discuss the entail or the will with you or the police.'

Rachel leant forward in her chair and said, 'Mr. Phipps, we do respect your discretion but I think you may feel differently if we told you, in complete confidence of course, that Lord Marbury was planning to change his will, or that is what he gave a close friend of his to believe, a day before someone tried to murder him.'

'Good Lord!'

'Quite. So you see, while we don't need to go into details, it would suffice for us to know whether it would have been possible for him to do so,' Jeremy responded.

'Well, of course, provided the change did not involve fee tailed land holdings and such. What Lord Marbury chooses to do with his un-entailed property and income from investments, which are quite significant on their own, is entirely up to him.'

Jeremy spoke. 'Let me make this clearer. What if, now this is merely speculation, Lord Marbury could legitimise an heir apparent over let's say, an heir presumptive, where would he stand legally? Could he change his will in favour of the former?'

'I don't really know. I've never given it much thought, in a manner of speaking. I don't think it's ever been done. But I suppose he could, provided the heir in question was not illegitimate.'

'And if we were to assume he was? My query is, has it ever been done, historically?'

'My dear man! That would depend entirely upon the legitimacy of the claim. Offhand I can only think of two very rare examples. There was the case of the Earl of Pembroke, eleventh if I'm not mistaken, who left his wealth and un-entailed property to a son by his second marriage as he had quarrelled with the heir apparent.'

'And the second?' Rachel piped up, 'You did mention two examples.'

'Yes, there was the fourth Marquess of Hertford who left several of properties and his very valuable art collection to his only child, Sir Richard Wallace who happened to be illegitimate, by the way. The now famous Wallace collection finds its roots there. But as you can see in both cases, the entailed property did go to the next in line officially. The Marquess' title and home – Ragley Hall and land holdings went to a distant connection, a cousin as far as I know.'

Jeremy said, 'I see. In that case I think I have a pertinent question. What is the rough valuation of Lord Marbury's un-entailed wealth, if I may ask?'

Mr. Phipps paused in reflection before he answered, 'As of last year, it was a quarter of a million pounds in investments alone apart from some valuable acquired artwork, jewellery, two new houses and an apartment block near Mayfair, altogether worth about another quarter of a million at the time of the last valuation.'

Jeremy whistled, 'I had no idea that on his own, that is without Marbury Hall and the entailed estates, he was worth that much. Half a million pounds makes for quite an impressive motive.'

'He was, pardon me, he is quite an industrious man. It is thanks to his efforts that when Mr. Pelham inherits Marbury Hall and the other properties, he will find himself in a tidy position of having self funding establishments. However, I must admit that without the Lordship's added personal wealth, he may find himself running a bit short on liquid cash. You see the entailed properties, this house, the other villas and townhouses cannot be sold or used commercially as per the estate's provision and must be preserved as is, to be handed down to the next generation.'

Rachel asked, 'But surely Lord Marbury must have made provisions for his wife and daughters and Mr. Pelham could not expect a bulk of his personal wealth to come to him?'

'I really don't know if I should be discussing this with you but under the circumstances, after what you've just told me, I feel it may have some relevance to your investigation.'

Rachel smiled, 'It can only help us, I assure you.'

'Apart from the use of the traditional dower house, Her Ladyship is to receive a house in Mayfair, fifty thousand pounds in investments along with some important pieces of jewellery and a sum of one hundred and fifty thousand pounds outright.'

'And the daughters?' Rachel queried.

'The daughters will receive a dowry of a hundred thousand pounds each along with some jewellery when they marry.'

'And the rest of Lord Marbury's personal wealth?' Jeremy asked.

'Apart from a few small bequests for staff, and a few charities here and there, the remainder, as things stand, goes to the heir, presumably Mr. Pelham along with the estate.'

Chapter Eleven

Mrs. Simmons came into the room shortly after Jeremy had accompanied Mr. Phipps out. She addressed Rachel pleasantly, 'Pardon me, madam. Might I have a word?'

Rachel looked up from the newspaper, 'Yes, Mrs. Simmons. How can I help you?'

'Well, it's just that a young lady has just turned up at the servant's hall claiming to be your lady's maid and since I've had no instructions regarding her arrival...'

'Good heavens! I completely forgot I'd rung for Betsy to join me after the sad incident with Summer. Do forgive me, Mrs. Simmons.'

At that moment the Countess entered the study and asked, 'Forgive you for what, my dear?'

'Oh, I am so glad you are here, Lady Marbury. I really ought to have asked your permission earlier. You see I'd rung my mother the other day to ask if she could send my maid up from Rutherford Hall. I thought it would be easier all around on your staff if I had my own maid sent up...'

The Countess responded with a smile, 'Say no more, my dear. I'm sure Mrs. Simmons will see to it that the girl is made comfortable.'

'Of course, your Ladyship!' Mrs. Simmons responded with a smile and left the room shutting the door behind her.

Rachel said, 'Thank you and I do apologise, Lady Marbury, for my forgetfulness.'

'Not at all. It used to be customary for most of our guests to bring their own maids and valets. I for one would be lost without mine when I travel. Although ever since the war, the custom has diminished somewhat. Servants are becoming harder to find or if Mrs. Simmons is to be believed, even harder to keep these days,' the Countess said with a smile.

Rachel nodded, 'I do admire your Mrs. Simmons. It must be quite a daunting task to run a household of this proportion.'

'Luckily for me, we inherited her along with the house. She has been in service here for over thirty years, as has our Butler. They were in the employ of the previous Earl and made a difficult transition easy for us. I have to admit that we've been very lucky where our staff is concerned. My own maid has been with me for nearly four and twenty years.'

'That is a long time by any standards.'

'She did abandon me about eighteen years ago to go and work at some factory or the other but she returned a year later and pleaded for her old position and I was quite happy to take her back. I've always thought it rather comforting to have a familiar face take care of my things. By the way, I did hear about your Schiaparelli and I am terribly sorry that we could not look after you better.'

'Please don't mention it, Lady Marbury. I'm sure I would not have had the heart to wear it ever again after what it witnessed, even if it wasn't ruined.'

'I agree. I'd feel the same way. Oh, look at me, just sitting and chatting away. I came in to ask you, if you and your husband would like a word with our gamekeeper, Mr. Hogan – the poor girl's father. Hobbs informed me that the man is waiting in the servant's hall. I could ask him to come up.'

'Thank you but no. I think it would probably be easier on him if we went down.'

II

As Jeremy and Rachel made their way past the sitting room, Ada Cellini's voice rang out, 'But André, you must listen to me!'

A young man's voice clipped back in a perfect British accent, 'I daresay you didn't have the time to play mother to me but I do wish you'd stop being so foreign and at least get my name right!'

'Don't be ashamed of your heritage. Remember you're only half English.'

He responded in an even voice. 'Yes and you never let me forget it, do you? Does it ever occur to you that apart from your genes, we have so little in common, Mother?'

'Santa Maria, save this boy!' Ada Cellini exclaimed dramatically lifting her hands to the Gods for help.

As Rachel and Jeremy paused and exchanged amused glances, Ada Cellini spotted them and she called out, 'There you are! Come and meet my son, André. I've just been telling him all about you. André, meet Mr. Richards and his wife. My dear I've forgotten your name. It's all very modern not taking on one's husband's name. It confuses people.'

Rachel smiled and quipped back, 'I daresay that is something we have in common, Madame Cellini for I have heard that your husband's name is Clayton.'

As they walked in, the red faced boy stood up to greet them. He was well built, casually dressed in tweed trousers and a black turtleneck. He had dark hair and a pale complexion which made the blush on his cheeks stand out more.

Madame Cellini spoke in her usual dramatic style. 'Ah, when you've changed husbands as many times as I have, one doesn't bother with changing one's name. I did it twice and got tired. Cellini was my second husband's name and Clayton is such a boring English name, like clay, like mud. Also as you know, I am famous. I think my admirers would not be happy if I kept confusing them, er...what is your name?'

'Rachel Markham, yet another boring English name,' she responded with a mischievous grin. Then turning to the young man she said, 'Pleased to meet you. This is my husband, Jeremy Richards.'

The young man made the effort to give an embarrassed laugh and said to Rachel, 'I hope you will ignore my mother's rudeness. I put it down to the Italian upbringing. She doesn't mean to be rude really.' Then he held out his hand to Jeremy. 'I'm Andrew Clayton, Mr. Richards. Very pleased to make your acquaintance.'

'Likewise, Mr. Clayton,' Jeremy responded shaking his hand.

'Please, call me Andrew. Everyone else does, well, apart from my mother, as I'm sure you've caught on by now.'

Ada Cellini gave a sigh and said, 'He was christened André when he was born but he is embarrassed by the name now, embarrassed that he is half Italian. Brainwashed by the British into thinking there is something wrong with one, if one is half foreign. Anglicised as my boy is, I simply do not understand why the English think they are a superior race. Their weather is miserable and the food even worse and their idea of culture begins and ends with Shakespeare. Pah! Look at what Italians have given to the world – the passion of Puccini, Verdi, Michaelangelo, Da Vinci, the Colosseum...'

Andrew interjected, 'Mother, please. This is not a contest. You are being tiresome...'

Rachel decided to intervene before the mother and son altercation heated up. 'Fact is, while we would love to stay and participate in this riveting conversation, we do have to meet someone downstairs. Please excuse us for the moment, Madame Cellini but we would like a word with you later on, if you don't mind, so please don't go away. We shall be back in two ticks.'

'I shall be ticking here,' Madame Cellini responded with a straight face as her son laughed out loud.

As Rachel and Jeremy left the room they heard her say, 'Ticks! Ha! What a language!'

'Mother, it's just a figure of speech! English is the language of Shakespeare, Lord Byron, Tennyson and...'

'Ha! I knew you would bring up Shakespeare!' As their voices faded, Rachel smiled to herself. She could still picture the two of them getting into another inevitable row on the merits and demerits of all things English. The irony of the fact that this conversation was taking place in the comfort of an old aristocratic English home, did not escape her.

Chapter Twelve

William Hogan, the gamekeeper was waiting patiently for them in the butler's pantry. He scraped back the wooden chair to get his bulk out of sitting position and greeted them gruffly. At 6'4" he towered over Rachel. She observed that he was in his fifties with a shock of unruly grey hair that had not seen a barber shop for at least six months. She noticed that his eyes, a sort of nondescript grey were too close together and his bushy moustache only just managed to balance his wide forehead, broad nose and square jaw. His clothes were like the man – shabby and unkempt.

Jeremy spoke. 'So sorry to have kept you waiting, Mr. Hogan but we were unavoidably detained by one of the guests.'

'Now't to worry about, sir. I'm used to waiting. Part of my job,' he said with a grave expression.

Rachel spoke as she took a chair, 'Mr. Hogan, at the outset I hope you will accept our condolences. I realise this must be a difficult time for you.'

'Aye, terrible thing to have happened. The poor little foundling,' he shook his head.

Rachel looked up in surprise. 'Pardon me, but I was given to believe that she was your daughter.'

'Nay, my wife and I brought her up as our own but she weren't our flesh and blood. My wife, Libby, God rest her soul, took her in when she were just about a month old. She told me that a friend of hers had died at childbirth and left summat for the girl's upbringing.'

'I am sorry, I had no idea, but I must say that was a very kind thing you did, Mr. Hogan. Please do take a seat,' Rachel responded with a smile.

As he sat back in his chair, Hogan spoke in a self-deprecating tone, 'Now't of the sort, Miss. Seeing as we had no bairns of our own, I thought it would keep the wife busy and out of my hair and it did. Besides, Libby told me that the child was already provided for so I had no problem with that. I didn't have much to do with her upkeep. T'was only after my wife died that I had to step in and get the girl a job as a housemaid up here at the big house. Poor 'un, she weren't too keen on it either. But the money left to her had run out long ago and I told her she was old enough to shift for herself.'

'I see. Your wife's passing must have been quite recent then? Summer informed me that she had just started working at the house two months ago,' Rachel observed.

'Aye, that's about right.'

Jeremy asked, 'If you don't mind my asking, how did your wife die, Mr. Hogan?'

'Well she drowned, didn't she, up by Burrough's Bridge. They said she lost her footing and fell into t'river. Never knew how to swim.'

'I see. And at the time, did the local police come up to investigate?' Jeremy asked.

'Aye. Said it was a tragic accident.'

'Did *you* think it was an accident?' Jeremy asked Hogan meaningfully and Rachel eyes widened in surprise.

Hogan answered simply, 'What else could it have been, sir?'

Jeremy responded, 'Oh, nothing, just getting our facts straight for now.'

Rachel asked, 'Mr. Hogan, are there any letters or papers that your wife may have left that will throw some light on who Summer's real parents were?'

'Don't think so. Well, I s'ppose you could go through Libby's things down at the cottage; I never got around to clearing 'em out but I can't see how it will help. The girl's parents, whoever they were are long dead and gone and a good thing too, with Summer being done in 'orribly like that.'

'Nevertheless, would you mind if I came by the cottage, sometime tomorrow morning and looked through their things?'

'Suit yourself, miss. I'll most likely be summat about in the woods. You'll find the key under the flowerpot by the door. Never bothered locking up before but we've had a bunch of odd blokes coming through the woods ever since the news of the Lordship's shooting went about.'

'Really? What sort of blokes?' Jeremy asked.

'Never seen 'em around these parts before, sir. Rough looking fellers. Spotted two of 'em just the other day. Told 'em I'd blow their heads off if I caught 'em prowlin' about the estate ever again.'

'And what did they have to say?' Jeremy asked with a tinge of amusement in his voice, as he realised that Hogan had managed to give Neville's thugs a taste of their own medicine.

'Well, sir, seeing as I had my loaded shotgun pointing at 'em they didn't have very much to say after all,' was Hogan's dry response.

II

Rachel was silent as they crossed the baize door into the family area of the house.

Jeremy said, 'You've gone very quiet, my dear.'

'Hmm...our little chat with Mr. Hogan has just given me a lot to think about. You do think his wife was murdered, don't you?'

'Well, there is a distinct possibility that her death may not have been accidental. In my experience, people who don't know how to swim are generally very careful around water bodies. Haven't come across very many cases where they conveniently fall into rivers and die. It just seems more likely that someone pushed her in.'

'I agree. But who do you think would have a motive in getting the gamekeeper's wife out of the way?'

Jeremy shrugged, 'If I had an answer to that, we'd be closer to solving this case. To my mind, the three incidents are too close together to be completely unrelated.'

'I can definitely understand why you think there is a connection between Summer's and her adoptive mother's deaths. All kinds of possibilities spring to mind, now that we know she was adopted.'

'Yes, we can't rule out a spot of blackmail gone wrong. Supposing André wasn't the only illegitimate child Lord Marbury sired and by Hogan's own admission the girl's money had run out...'

'But then where does Lord Marbury's attempted murder fit into the equation? If one assumes that they were the blackmailers and he was the "blackmailee" why shoot him? I still don't get the connection.'

'Now that is something we need to find out.'

'But Jeremy, the blackmail theory has too many holes in it. Firstly, the adoptive mother was already dead by the time of the Earl's shooting. Secondly, the man in question is in a comatose state and could not have had any role to play in Summer's murder.'

'I'll admit it's all a muddle at the moment but we need to find out who the girl's birth parents were. I think I'll go into the village tomorrow and send out some telegrams while you rummage through the cottage. We need to get access to two sets of birth records.'

'That sounds sensible enough, if they haven't been blitzed in the war!'

'Quite the optimist, aren't you?' Jeremy said with good natured sarcasm.

'If you ask me, you are the real optimist here, Mister. After all, we can't be sure that the first death wasn't an accident and in all possibility there may be no connection whatsoever between the Earl's shooting and the maid's murder!'

'I know this may sound daft but I can feel it in my bones. There is definitely some connection even if we can't see it straight away.' Jeremy said with conviction.

'Well then, let's hope that my visit to the cottage will throw some light on to this dark affair.'

Jeremy nodded. 'Yes. In the meantime, I think it's time we got Tosca to sing for her supper.'

III

By the time Rachel and Jeremy returned to the sitting room, the rest of the family and house guests had gathered in the sitting room awaiting the lunch gong, which was expected to go off in fifteen minutes. People were scattered about the room and the hum of polite conversation wafted around them.

Jeremy made his way to Madame Cellini's side and said, 'We are so glad you are still here. We'd like a word with you alone in Lord Marbury's study, if you don't mind.'

The soprano asked, 'Why alone? Why all the secrecy? Why can't we talk here?' as she languidly reclined further into the sofa cushions. She took a puff from her long cigarette holder and blew out curls of blue smoke towards Jeremy.

Rachel responded patiently in a soft voice, 'Madame, the matter we wish to discuss is somewhat of a delicate nature. We don't have a problem discussing it here but it may cause some embarrassment for you.'

'Embarrassment for me?' She asked loudly with a laugh looking around at the people in the room. 'Why? Have the great detectives come to the conclusion that I shot Magnus?'

'Did you?' Rachel couldn't resist retorting.

'Certainly not and if I did do you think I would tell you? What was your name again?'

Rachel answered wearily, 'My name was and still is Rachel. Perhaps I should wear a name card around my neck for your benefit. Oh, never mind that. Are you quite sure you want to be questioned in here?'

'My dear, unlike you English girls, I do not blush at everything in life. I do not fear embarrassment, I have nothing to hide,' she said in a loud voice with her signature flamboyance.

Rachel shrugged and said in an equally loud voice, 'In that case what we would like to ask you is – who is André's real father?'

Suddenly there was a hush in the room and all eyes were on them. Rachel realised that she had allowed the woman to goad her into overstepping her own set bounds of decency. And it was too late to take it back.

There was a pause. Then the prima donna glared back at her and roared, 'How dare you? Who are you, a little nobody from nowhere to ask *me* something like that?'

Andrew Clayton stood up. 'I say, this isn't quite cricket.'

Baron Braybourne gave a short cough and came to Rachel's rescue, 'My dear, I've been meaning to share something with you both in private, if you'd care to step this way,' he said holding the connecting door to the study open.

Rachel walked through the door followed by Jeremy who whispered in her ear, 'Well, that certainly went well, don't you think?'

Rachel gave him a withering look but said no more as the Baron closed the door behind them.

The three of them stood silently as he walked to the decanter stand and asked with a smile, 'Brandy anyone?'

Rachel shook her head and Jeremy followed suit.

The Baron poured the remnants of the decanter into a glass and raised a toast, 'To discreet detectives and their methods!'

Jeremy mumbled, 'Hear, hear!' under his breath as the Baron took a large sip. Before Rachel could respond, his face turned red as his hand went to his throat and he made a choking sound before he keeled over, gurgling, 'Poison. Call the doctor...I...I can't breathe...I think this brandy...is poisoned.'

Rachel rushed ahead to help him while Jeremy opened the connecting door to the sitting room, shouting for help.

Chapter Thirteen

Just after sun down, Dr. Farnsworth was enclosed in the study with the members of the house party. Andrew Clayton and Roderick Cartwright stood by the fireplace while Lady Marbury, Miranda and Lady Stephanie were seated on the settee. Neville Pelham, Lady Claire and Rachel were seated in armchairs opposite them. Jeremy and Adam Brabazon stood reclining against the desk in the study. Ada Cellini had taken to her bed and was conspicuous in her absence.

The doctor spoke. 'It's quite an unusual poison. I have sent the decanter and the glass for chemical analysis to a London laboratory, however I have no doubt that the results will show that it contained a large concentration of atropine, hyoscine and hyoscyamine derived from a rather toxic plant commonly known as the deadly nightshade.'

'Is my father going to be alright?' Roderick asked nervously.

'We've given him strong emetics and pumped the stomach, apart from giving him a shot of physostigmine commonly called pilocarpine, which is the only known antidote for atropine poisoning. He will need rest and depending on his constitution, he may suffer for a day or two from palpitations, rashes, discomfort and perhaps even hallucinations but yes he will be fine. Lucky for him that he didn't have a heart condition in which case it could have proven fatal.'

Jeremy spoke. 'I'll say! Extremely lucky for him that you managed to pinpoint which poison had been used even before the results of the chemical analysis came in.'

The doctor responded. 'More serendipity than luck really. Last September, I treated three children from the village for similar symptoms. Unfortunately the youngest of the lot, a five year old died. They had gone for a walk in the woods and eaten the berries from the plant. Extremely toxic. In this case, I could tell immediately because one of the most visible symptoms of this particular poison is an extreme dilation of the pupils. And by a stroke of good fortune, I happened to have had a stock of physostigmine left over from the previous case, in my dispensary.'

Rachel asked, 'You mentioned atropine. Isn't it used in eye drops?'

'Yes but never in this concentration. No, the poison must have been administered from a highly concentrated tincture distilled from the deadly nightshade or belladonna, as it better known in the continent.'

Miranda spoke, 'Did you just say belladonna? In that case I do believe Rachel could have a valid point. I have a vague recollection of belladonna being used historically by Italian women and later by our Victorian ancestors to dilate their pupils. Made them more attractive to the opposite sex or so they thought. Catherine, don't you remember back at finishing school we experimented with it?'

The Countess' response was vague, 'Did we?'

'Of course we did! And I remember our pupils became enormous. My God! That explains it! If I'm not mistaken, I think Ada still uses the stuff. One only has to look into her eyes to know that she does.'

Andrew Clayton spoke indignantly, 'I say, are you suggesting my mother had anything to do with poisoning Lord Braybourne?'

Jeremy addressed him in an even tone, 'Mr. Clayton, please calm down. No one is suggesting anything yet. But if your mother does happen to possess a tincture of belladonna concentrate, we would need to find out if it has been used by a person or persons yet unknown, to poison the Baron.'

Rachel shook her head and said slowly as if she had just had a revelation. 'I don't want to put a cat amongst your pigeons, darling, but I can't help thinking we've got it the other way round. It seems far more likely to me that the Baron inadvertently drank the poisoned brandy which was meant for us.'

There was a hush in the room as Rachel's words sank in. She added meaningfully, looking at those present one by one, 'After all, I am quite sure that everyone in this room is aware that we got Lady Marbury's permission this morning, to begin conducting our investigation from this very room.'

Miranda raised an eyebrow, as she addressed Rachel, 'I can't speak for the others but from that little exhibition earlier on, it seemed evident to me that you, my dear, are definitely not one of Ada's favourite people.'

Andrew Clayton flared up, 'I say! How dare you insinuate...'

Miranda snapped at him, 'Oh, do shut up Andrew. We all know there is a homicidal maniac on the loose here. Politeness be damned. I'm going upstairs right now to find out where your mother's tincture of belladonna is.'

II

'Well, of course I use belladonna...everyone in the opera does! Go and look, the drops are on my dresser!' Ada Cellini bellowed after having been rudely shaken out of her nap by Miranda and Rachel. She put on a silk dressing gown as the men requested her permission to enter her boudoir.

Miranda walked to the chintz covered dresser and pushed aside the ivory backed hair brushes. She then sat on the chair and Rachel noticed that she pulled something towards her. On closer inspection, it was the ornate silver tray holding various glass bottles containing perfumes, presumably other beauty anointments and scented lotions. After rummaging through them, Miranda picked a small green bottle with a drop stopper, and holding it up to the light, she said, 'Ada is right and it seems to be here, quite full up too.'

Dr. Farnsworth walked to her, took the bottle in his hand and unscrewed the dropper top and sniffed. 'Yes. But this is diluted. Can't possibly have been used to poison Lord Braybourne. What he ingested was far more concentrated.' Then turning to Ada, he asked, 'Madame, is it possible you have a bottle of belladonna concentrate too?'

Ada replied, 'Yes, it should be somewhere there too, a little brown bottle. You can't get it here so I buy it from a trusted source in Rome, everytime I perform there.'

Jeremy spoke, 'May we have a look at it?'

Ada walked over to the dresser and said, 'It's a brown bottle with a cork stopper. It should be here.'

Miranda shook her head, 'Well, it's not here now.'

Ada said as she slapped her forehead, 'Ah, of course, how foolish of me. I'll ring for the maid, I forget her name. It's probably still with her. She mixed the last bottle for me. It's one part belladonna...'

The doctor intercepted, 'To a hundred parts sterile water.'

Ada looked up, 'Quite right, yes.'

Rachel asked, 'When did you last ask her to mix it?'

'The day before, I think,' Ada responded.

Jeremy asked, 'And do you know where she mixed it?'

Ada replied, 'In the kitchen of course, where else?'

Jeremy said slowly, 'I see, so the kitchen staff would've had access to it?'

'I don't know, I suppose so,' she said with a shrug.

There was a knock on the door and Tilly entered, 'You rang, madam?'

Ada looked irritated as she spoke, 'Yes but I rang for the girl who's been attending to me. I don't want you!'

'Well, madam, I'm afraid, Ivy is missing so Mrs. Simmons asked me to look in...'

Rachel asked unable to avoid the alarm in her voice, 'Missing? What do you mean missing?'

'We can't find her anywhere, madam. It's like she's disappeared.'

Dr. Farnsworth sighed and said, 'I think we had better ring for the police.'

III

The police arrived shortly and a search party was duly formed to look for the missing girl. It was cold and dark outside. Snow had been falling steadily all afternoon and the visibility was poor. A blizzard had been predicted. The footmen led the way with torches. Even with the torch light; they could barely see a thing. The men of the house had formed two groups; one to fan out and comb through the estate and grounds; and the other to the woods beyond. Only Hobbs had been left behind.

In the servant's hall, voices were raised. Amidst the din Myrtle's voice rang out, 'It's like a blooming epidemic it is!'

'You mean, we're not safe either?' Nora asked in a panic stricken voice.

Myrtle sniggered, 'What d'you think, you ha'porth, first Summer, now Ivy...'

Mr. Hobbs came in and spoke in his authoritative voice, 'What's all this, I hear?'

The maids went quiet in his presence.

Mary spoke up in her tremulous voice, 'Myrtle here was just saying that we're likely to be murdered in our beds, if we stay on, Mr. Hobbs!'

Mr. Hobbs gave her a look of cold disdain and said, 'Nobody is going to be murdered in their beds – not on my watch. And meanwhile, I would appreciate it, if you all stopped behaving as though you were raised in a barn. Now...'

Myrtle interrupted his flow, 'But, Mr. Hobbs, Ivy didn't go on her own. She would have told me something if...'

Hobbs cut her short in his sonorous voice, 'I'm sure there is a perfectly reasonable explanation why Ivy is not here, and I am certain that Mrs. Simmons will share it with you all, as soon as she hears something. Now if there are no further interruptions, I would like to know, who is Betsy?'

Betsy pushed back her chair and stood up, 'I am, sir.'

'Well, Miss Betsy, since I haven't had the honour of being knighted yet, you may refer to me as Mr. Hobbs. More to the point, Mrs. Simmons has just sent word that you are wanted upstairs. Myrtle, could you kindly show her up to Mrs. er...Madam Markham's room.'

'Certainly, Mr. Hobbs,' Myrtle responded as she got up.

'As for the rest of you, let's get back to work, shall we,' Hobbs said as the maids stood up and the tweenies and kitchen maids scrambled to get back to their duties.

As Betsy and Myrtle made their way out of the servants' hall, Betsy asked, 'You shared a room with Ivy, didn't you?'

Myrtle answered, 'Yes and that's what's bothering me. I mean, if she did go off somewhere, as Mr. Hobbs suggests, she would have taken some of her things.'

'I quite agree.'

'That's what is so peculiar. I checked while the police were looking about and all her things are still there, even her toothbrush! If you ask me, she's been done in just like that poor Summer.'

'Well, that remains to be seen. You oughtn't to jump to conclusions just yet.'

'Oh, oughtn't I, now? Well, you needn't get all hoity-toity with us just yet, missy. You just got here. What do you know 'bout anything?'

'I am sorry. I didn't mean to upset you. Did Ivy seem nervous to you the past few days?'

'What a question! We've all been nervous the past few days, ever since Summer was found with her head bashed in. Made us wonder who'd be next.'

Chapter Fourteen

Rachel closed the door to her room behind them. 'Thank goodness we've been left alone, Betsy. How are you getting on downstairs, then?'

'Oh, miss, there was an awful kerfuffle about the girl's disappearance. But I haven't uncovered anything yet. They all seem to be scared out of their wits but no one has a clue about what's going on. If anyone does, they're not letting on.'

'Give it time and try and get chummy with the other girls.'

'I wish it were that easy, miss. As it is, I think I've managed to rub one or two of them the wrong way already.'

'Oh dear, but don't worry; if you keep your eyes and ears open downstairs, you may be able to get insights that we can't. So keep at it.'

'Yes, miss.'

'What do you know so far about this girl – Ivy?'

'Nothing much yet, except that she didn't take anything with her.'

'Can you get into her room and look about for yourself? I don't know what we're looking for exactly but you know, anything like notes, letters or even a hiding place that the police may have overlooked.'

'I'll try, miss. She shares her room with another girl. As soon as I get the chance, I'll do it.'

'Betsy, promise me you will be careful.'

'Of course I will, miss,' Betsy replied sounding nonchalant.

'It isn't like the last time you helped me catch a killer, you know. This time I'm not sure what we're up against, people are being shot at and poisoned; a girl has been murdered and another has already gone missing, so I want you to keep your eyes peeled and your wits about you, do you understand?'

'Don't worry, miss. I don't much fancy the idea of being done in, myself,' Betsy said with a grin.

'Glad to hear it. Oh, and I almost forgot. Two of the girls reported hearing someone walk about in the corridor of the maids sleeping quarters in the middle of the night. Their theory is that it's a ghost but of course I think that's all my eye and then some. If you hear anything, I don't want you to take any unwanted risks but...' Rachel lowered her voice to a whisper, 'if you could just take a peek at who it is without getting caught...'

'If someone's walking about, I'll be on to them like billy-o, don't you worry, miss,' Betsy informed her cheerfully.

'Hmm, that is precisely what worries me,' Rachel said, rolling her eyes.

There was a knock at the door and Jeremy entered. 'I thought I heard voices. Hello Betsy.'

'Good evening, sir, I was just leaving.'

'Right. We'll see you about then,' he said, as he made his way to the fireplace.

After Betsy left shutting the room door behind her, Rachel asked, 'Any news? Did you find any trace of the girl? Anything at all?'

'Afraid not. Couldn't see our hands in front of our faces. The blizzard has set in and it's freezing out there.'

'Goodness, darling, you do look like an icicle. Take off your wet things and thaw out.'

'I hope the girl has gone into hiding, preferably somewhere warm. We know she didn't go into the village or take the train. The station master is certain of that. But I wouldn't give much for her chances if she is wandering about in the wilderness in this godforsaken weather.'

'Poor thing. I wonder what could've frightened her into taking flight like that.'

'Charles, the footman did say that he saw her drop a tray when they went downstairs right after the doctor's visit. According to him she looked as white as a sheet when she heard the news that Lord Braybourne was poisoned with belladonna.'

'I see. And according to Ada, she was the last person who had the bottle of belladonna. I wonder...' Rachel said reflectively. And then she sprang into action. 'I shan't be a minute, darling but I forgot to ask Betsy something,' she said as she ran out of the room into the corridor.

She caught up with Betsy as she turned into the main corridor. There was no one else about.

Betsy looked at her with astonishment, 'What is it, miss?'

Rachel held her arm and said between breaths, 'Her coat. Ask that girl who rooms with Ivy, I've forgotten her name...'

'Myrtle?'

'Yes, that's it, Myrtle. Ask her to check if she's taken her coat.'

'Her coat, miss?' Betsy asked puzzled.

'Yes, you told me that Ivy took nothing with her. But ask her to look again and see if Ivy's coat is still there.'

'I'll do that. And I may not need to check with Myrtle for that. The servant's coats and hats usually hang on the hooks in the back passageway.'

'Yes, all the same, you'll probably need her help in identifying her things.'

'Alright, miss. Should I report back to you now or in the morning?'

'Now, please. I'll sleep a lot better if I know her coat is gone.'

As Rachel turned around she heard the sound of another door opening somewhere behind her. Tilly, the

Countess' maid came out on to the corridor carrying a package wrapped in brown paper. She acknowledged her as she passed by, 'Goodnight, madam.'

Rachel smiled back, 'Goodnight. By the way, isn't that Lord Braybourne's room I saw you coming out of?'

'Yes, madam. Her ladyship asked me to pack some of his things to take to the hospital.'

'But isn't that supposed to be the valet's job?' Rachel asked.

Tilly shrugged, 'His valet must be at the hospital.'

'Yes, of course, well goodnight,' Rachel said as she walked back to her room, giving it no further thought.

Ten minutes later, an excited Betsy came into the room and said, 'You were right, miss. Her coat's gone along with her gloves and hat.'

Jeremy looked up from the book he was reading by the fireplace, as Rachel answered, 'Ah, thank you, Betsy for being the bearer of good tidings. I shall sleep easier tonight.'

'What was all that about?' Jeremy asked as the girl left.

'At least we know now that Ivy left on her own accord and isn't lying murdered somewhere like poor Summer was, before I discovered her body.'

'Yes she may have left of her own accord but that isn't reason enough to believe that she is safe.'

'We'll cross that bridge when we get to it in the morning, darling. For now that bit of news is enough for me. She's probably safer out of the house than in it.'

'You're being very cryptic. Do you know something that I don't?'

'Not yet but I promise you will be the first to know when I do.'

'Hmm then why am I suddenly getting a sense of déjà vu? I can only hope you are not planning to attempt anything dangerous. That warehouse episode in Paris still haunts me.'

'There you can rest easy, my love. There aren't any warehouses here, not for miles and miles,' Rachel replied with a cheeky grin.

'Thank goodness for small mercies,' Jeremy deadpanned back.

'That reminds me. I had better get my revolver out of the suitcase in the luggage room tomorrow morning,' Rachel said, thinking aloud.

'And *that* is all I needed to hear. Unless you want to be under house arrest, young lady, you had better spill the beans now!'

Rachel laughed and responded, 'There's no use bullying me into answering just yet, darling. I'll let you know as soon as I find out, that is if I'm right. Now I'm going to bed. Tomorrow looks like it's going to be a long day.'

'My fears, exactly. Good night, darling.'

Chapter Fifteen

Rachel was up by eight in the morning, minutes before the Sun made its own feeble attempt to dispel the darkness. She gazed out through the windows in her room as she dressed by the firelight. The blizzard had carpeted everything in white the night before and although it had stopped snowing, the leaden skies looked as though they promised to cover the land with a fresh blanket of snow before long, so she chose to clad herself warmly. Despite the gloom in the sky, she was all set to make the most of her day. Jeremy was still asleep as she went down for breakfast and met Neville Pelham and Adam Brabazon in the dining hall.

'You boys are up bright and early,' she said as she greeted them.

Neville smiled weakly as Adam responded, 'I don't know about bright but you are quite right about early.

The chauffeur is down with the flu, poor lad, and now Neville, so I have the honour of driving Lady Marbury, Aunt Miranda and the girls for their bi-weekly visits to the hospital.'

Neville sneezed as if on cue and spoke through his handkerchief in a muffled voice, 'I don't envy you. It looks like snow, you know.'

Adam responded, 'Which is why we thought we'd make an early start and get back before the weather turns for the worse.'

Neville nodded. 'Quite right, old chap. As it is I feel quite guilty about asking you to step in and take over the bally driving duty last minute but it can't be helped. I'm feeling terribly under the weather myself.'

Adam responded laughingly, 'Don't worry your pretty little head over it. You just take rest and get some beauty sleep. God knows you need it!' Neville grinned back at him and pulled a face.

Lady Claire walked in adjusting her gloves. She was smartly dressed in a cream and black coat and a stylish hat to match. 'All set, Adam? Mama will be down soon.'

Adam replied between mouthfuls, 'Just finishing up here. Won't you have some breakfast?'

'Stephanie and I had our breakfast trays brought up earlier so we could be ready on time. We've rather let go of the old customs,' she said smiling at Rachel. Then looking at Neville she spoke in her usual imperious way, 'I gather we can trust you, Neville, to keep our guests amused while we are away.'

'Well, I err...' Neville spluttered as Rachel came to his rescue and spoke, 'I daresay, Lady Claire that won't be necessary. My husband plans to go into the village today to send out some telegrams and I have some things to do on my own so...'

Lady Claire nodded back and said, 'Well, he could take a ride with Madame Cellini. I believe she is taking Lord Braybourne's car into the village later on to run some errands but of course she is a late riser and he might have to wait a while.'

Rachel responded with a smile, 'Oh, I'm sure he wouldn't want to bother Madame Cellini but it is kind of you to mention it.'

Lady Claire said, 'Right, well, ask Hobbs to ring for the village taxicab. There's no point in your husband trying to walk to the village. He'll probably lose his way with everything covered in snow.'

Rachel nodded, 'That is a good suggestion. Thank you. And I've been meaning to ask, is there any news on the girl who went missing last night?'

Lady Claire responded, 'I'm afraid not. Although, I'm sure something will turn up. The Constable is on his way I'm told. They are planning to continue with the search.'

'Right,' Rachel said contemplatively.

'Well then, we'll see you when we get back. Chop-chop, Adam, I think I can hear Mama out in the hall,' she said as she sashayed out of the room.

Adam pushed back his chair, leaving his breakfast half eaten as he gave Rachel a grimace and followed Lady Claire out into the hall.

II

Half an hour later, Rachel saw Jeremy off at the main entrance, as he left for the village post office in the taxicab. Glancing about her, she noticed that the predicted blizzard had well and truly set in. Undeterred, Rachel decided to ask Mrs. Simmons for help in locating the gamekeeper's cottage in the woods. Billy, the boot boy was duly bundled up in several layers and appointed to show her the way. Fifteen minutes later Rachel and the bundle were walking as briskly as they could through the snow flurry. He showed her the markings of the path now obliterated by the snow. Fragile branches snapped under the weight of their icy white burdens and fell about them as they walked on the path leaving two sets of footprints on the fresh white carpet laid out for them.

They walked in silence for about ten minutes. On any given day, a walk through the woods always gave her great pleasure but today as the small, quaint old cottage covered in snow came into view through the trees, there was an added surreal beauty about the picture and Rachel found herself awash in childlike wonder and a sense of enchantment. Almost as though she had walked into a life sized snow globe, just like the one she had treasured ever since she was a child – a cherished Christmas gift from her grandfather.

As she gazed up at the picturesque cottage, she noticed that parts of the ivy that covered the cottage had broken away from the wall, probably under the weight of the recent snow.

Billy stomped up to the door and banged on it simultaneously hollering at the top of his voice,

'Mr. Hogan! You've got a visitor. Mr. Hogan? Are you there? Anybody there? Hello! Mr. Hogan?'

Rachel shook her head and said, 'That's alright Billy. You can stop shouting now. That was loud enough to wake the dead. I don't think Mr. Hogan is in after all.' She started lifting the smaller flowerpots to look for the key.

Billy grinned at her and retorted, 'In this weather? He'd be a daft beggar, to be out.'

'Well, we're out, aren't we?'

'Don't make us no less daft!'

Rachel grinned back. 'Never mind that. Ah! I've found the key. Let's get in and make ourselves a cup of tea. I'm sure Mr. Hogan won't mind.'

'I wonder where he could've gone. I don't reckon we'll get any poachers hereabouts, not with the snow and all.'

Rachel said, 'I suspect he must've gone to check on his traps or some such thing, whatever gamekeepers do on a regular basis in the woods.'

'Aye, ma'am,' he nodded as Rachel turned the key and he followed her in.

The cheerful lace trimmed curtains visible from outside had given her a misleading impression. She was expecting a comfortable and cosy cottage on the inside. Instead as she looked about the dark and dingy low ceilinged room, she realised with dismay that Hogan lived a very rustic lifestyle. His late wife must have been responsible for the lace trimmings on the curtains and framed embroideries that were scattered on the walls. There were wooden beams jutting out from the ceiling and a tall man like Hogan would have to stoop in order to avoid bumping his head. In that sense it was cosy but there was nothing cosy about the smell of stale tobacco mingled with the stench of rancid food which permeated the closed atmosphere.

The room brightened a bit as Billy lit the paraffin lamp hanging near the door. Rachel spotted an iron pan suspended over a rod in the fireplace. Probably last night's stew, she thought to herself as she wrinkled up her nose. There was clutter everywhere. Wooden logs were stacked haphazardly up on the wall next to the stone fireplace. Opposite it sat a much used chintz sofa that had seen better days and now had a dirty rug thrown over it. Two basic wooden chairs were against the wall next to it. A narrow staircase led up to what she presumed were the sleeping quarters.

On the other end of the room, a large battered old table stood near an old Aga. It looked as though Hogan used it as an all-in-one kitchen countertop cum dining table. A near empty bottle of local whiskey stood next to the half full bottle of milk on the table and as she could see no glasses or mugs near it, she realised Hogan probably drank straight from the bottle. A sideboard with shelves was strewn with pots and miscellaneous odds and ends, half a loaf of bread, a broken ceramic jug and various tins of food items along with a tin of Players Navy Cut tobacco. There was a basin next to the window with a wooden bucket to hold the water for washing up. She spotted the kettle on a shelf but as she didn't know where she could get running water from she told Billy that tea was no longer on offer. He said he could bring in some water from the hand pump out back near the outdoor privy, if it hadn't frozen over and make some for her. Rachel declined his kind offer.

She shuddered inwardly. An outdoor privy, no wonder Hogan looked so unkempt. If she had to clean any part of herself with icy cold water, she would probably end up looking like him too. She knew that thousands of people still lived like this in villages dotted all over the countryside but what surprised her was that the cottage was so close to the splendour and opulent luxury of Marbury Hall, yet people living on the same estate grounds lived without basic amenities such as electricity, running water or in house bathrooms, things she herself took for granted.

Getting her mind back to the task on hand she told Billy that she needed to check the rooms upstairs and as they trudged up the narrow wooden stairs, and reached the tiny first floor landing, they heard a distinct sound of a floorboard creaking above as though someone had just walked across.

Billy looked up and said, 'Blimey! There's somebody up in the attic.'

Chapter Sixteen

'Shh!' Rachel said putting a finger on her lips. She whispered to him, 'You stay here, Billy, while I go up and see who it is.'

Billy whispered back in a panic, 'What if it's the murderer? What if he murders you next?'

Rachel raised an eyebrow. 'Fat chance. I've got a gun,' she whispered back as she reached into her overcoat pocket and brought out her ivory inlaid Colt 380 with a dramatic flourish.

'Cor lumme!' was Billy's admiration laden response.

As Rachel gingerly made her way up the step-ladder to the attic, they heard a piece of heavy furniture being dragged over the trapdoor. Whoever was up there was taking no chances. Rachel banged on the trapdoor and said loudly, 'We know you are up there. You can't stay cooped in forever. Come down and talk to us. You have nothing to fear.'

Billy added his own reassuring two bits by hollering, 'Aye and no funny tricks, mind. The lady's got a gun!'

Rachel rolled her eyes. The next thing they heard was a banging sound which sounded suspiciously like the flapping of a window pane against the wind.

Rachel cursed. 'Damn! There must be a window up there. Quick, boy get down. Our intruder is getting away.'

'He'll break his neck, he will!'

'Not if he's an expert at clambering up and down the ivy! I suspect that's how he probably got in, in the first place,' she said remembering the broken ivy she had spotted earlier.

A few minutes later, they were outside as the howling wind and snow whipped about them. A fresh set of running footprints were visible on the side of the cottage as the intruder had made his getaway into the woods. Rachel knew there was no point in following this person into the woods in this weather. The footprints would get covered in no time and then they would end up achieving nothing. She told Billy to get back inside as she took a closer look at the footprints. She made a mental note of the vertical markings made by the sole, so that she could give an accurate description to the constabulary later.

Two minutes later, she was back inside the cottage. The Colt was back inside her pocket and she was determined to finish what she came here to do in the first place - go through Libby's and Summer's things. She told Billy to keep a watch from the downstairs windows, in case the intruder returned. She then went upstairs to commence her investigation.

There were two doors on the landing. Opening the first one, she realised it was Hogan and Libby's room. It was cluttered and smelt musty. She decided she would come back to it later. She closed that door and opened the door to the second room. This was smaller and in all likelihood had been Summer's room. There was a narrow bedstead, a bedside table and a chest of drawers with a ceramic basin and jug sitting on top. There was also a small mirror behind the jug with some toiletries in front of it. A lipstick case, a jar of cold cream, a hair brush, some bobby pins, a tiny flacon of perfume and a new soap tin. She walked to it and opened the lipstick case and twisted it up. It was a bright red shade and it looked as though Summer had recently gone shopping with her wages. The other toiletries looked new as well.

The bed had not been made and there were some items of clothing on it. A pair of new black shoes stood under the bed. Rachel got a catch in her throat as she realised that it looked as though the occupant was just out for the day. It was almost as if the room was waiting for its occupant to come back home and claim it, which only served to bring back vivid images of finding Summer, her young life snuffed out, her body heartlessly stuffed into the laundry basket. Rachel felt a shudder go through her, as though someone had just walked over her bones. She berated herself for being morbid and decided to look for papers, letters anything she could find that would give her a clue to solving Summer's murder.

Just as she opened the first chest of drawers, she heard Billy running up the stairs. He rushed in wide eyed and said, 'Miss, I think the murderer is coming back. A man is walking towards the house and it ain't Mr. Hogan.'

They heard the front door open and shut. Rachel motioned him to keep quiet and hide on the other side of the chest of drawers. She herself shut the room door as quietly as possible and took up position behind it with the gun in her hand as they heard steady footsteps ascending the stairs. If the intruder was indeed coming back, he probably meant business this time. Rachel could feel her heart beating like a drum against her chest.

The footsteps halted on the landing outside and then as though in slow motion she saw the ceramic knob turn as the door opened slowly. She could smell the man's cologne even before his back came into view. She knew who it was.

As the man took a step towards the bed, Rachel stepped behind him and said calmly, 'Hands up, Mr. Pelham. I've got a gun. If you do anything idiotic, I shan't hesitate to blow your head off.'

The man whirled about in surprise and Rachel's gun went off in the air.

Pelham dived to the floor, yelling, 'Stop shooting! Are you mad? What are you doing here? Put the blasted gun down.'

Rachel didn't lose her wits. She walked closer to him and pointed the revolver at his chest and asked in a steely voice, 'More to the point Mr. Pelham, what are you doing here, in Summer's room?'

'Look. I just came here to retrieve some er... personal correspondence, some letters, alright?'

'Right, show me the soles of your shoes. Now!'

'What? Why?'

'Just do as you're told and nobody gets hurt.'

'Alright suit yourself. Here. Happy now?' He said displaying one of the soles.

Rachel noted that apart from being larger, his shoes had a zigzag pattern on the soles that bore no resemblance to the footprints made by the intruder.

'I apologise, Mr. Pelham. You gave us a scare that's all. Billy, you can come out now. It's not the same person.'

Pelham shouted, 'I gave you a scare? What do you mean, I gave you a scare? You damn nearly killed me waving your gun about like that. You'll be lucky if I don't press charges. I say, do you even have a licence for that thing?'

'Nice try, Mr. Pelham. Why don't we just wait here for Mr. Hogan to return and then we'll see who presses charges against whom. I don't suppose he even knows you're here and something tells me he isn't going to be too chuffed about finding you in his daughter's room, attempting to steal her correspondence.'

'Let's be reasonable, shall we? I was a bit, how can I put it... well, indiscreet and now that the poor girl is, well you know...'

'Yes, I do know. I found her body, remember?' Rachel reminded him and then looking at Billy's wide eyed gaze, she addressed the boy, 'Billy, why don't you wait downstairs for me? Mr. Pelham and I need to talk.'

As Billy left the room, Neville said plaintively, 'I ask you, what harm is there, if I retrieve the letters,

I myself wrote to her? It would save everyone a lot of embarrassment.'

Rachel responded, 'That would be akin to tampering with evidence in a murder case, Mr. Pelham.'

'Surely, you can't suspect me? I was very fond of the girl, perhaps a bit more than I should have been but there it is.'

Rachel raised an eyebrow at this revelation and Neville continued sheepishly, 'Alright, truth is, we were lovers but I would never have hurt a hair on her head. I did love her you know.'

'More crimes have been committed in the name of love than anything else. Perhaps she threatened to reveal the true nature of your alliance to Lady Claire and you killed her to save yourself from the aforementioned embarrassment.'

'Look, if you think I killed Summer, then I can't talk to you. I have nothing more to say,' he said looking crestfallen.

The sincerity in his voice gave Rachel a turn as she realised that he was telling the truth. Whatever else he was guilty of, he was not Summer's killer.

She relented, 'Alright, be my guest. Look for your letters. You can have them on one condition – I want to see their content before you cart them off. Just to make sure that they are exactly what you claim they are.'

'Done. Thank you!' Then on second thought, he asked, 'Are you just going to sit here and watch me?'

'Like a hawk. Yes, I am,' she said smugly, as she sat down on the edge of the lumpy bed and he started to go through the chest of drawers.

The search proved unfruitful. The chest of drawers did have some papers but they turned out to be bills and some newspaper clippings on fashion and dress patterns. Rachel checked under the lumpy mattress and found a flat old biscuit tin wedged between the bed and the bedpost which contained some old black and white photographs with captions on the back. Some dated back to 1914. Neville looked elated until he realised that the box contained only old photographs and nothing else. There was no sign of his letters. While he was looking the other way, Rachel slipped the slim box in her overcoat pocket. She wanted to go through the photographs at leisure before handing it back to Mr. Hogan. They moved to the next room and searched there as well but the letters were nowhere to be found. Finally after going through the contents of every single tin and box in the room below they gave up. The only option left was the attic and the trapdoor was barred by a heavy object.

Neville tried to bribe Billy into climbing up the ivy and removing the piece of furniture but the boy had had enough excitement for one day and turned his offer down flat. Rachel congratulated Billy on allowing good sense to prevail as she felt that it was far too dangerous in this weather. A glance out the windows showed her that the blizzard had taken a turn for the worse. The three of them decided to call it quits before it became worse. Being stranded in this dingy icebox of a cottage was not a prospect that appealed to any of them.

If the cottage had been cold, it was nothing compared to the walk back to the Hall. As she stepped out locking the cottage door and replacing the key under the flowerpot, she sent up a silent prayer for the intruder and anyone else who was caught out in this sudden blast from the arctic. They walked slowly bracing themselves against the bitter cold as icy wind slapped against them. Her snow globe had turned completely white – with just three lone figures wading through the fast forming snow drifts, their breath turning to frost.

Chapter Seventeen

Back at the Hall, Rachel went straight to her room, rung for Betsy and began peeling off her wet things. Betsy brought up a hot water bottle and added some logs to the fireplace to get the fire going again. Then she helped Rachel dry her hair and change into her warmest cashmere dress.

Rachel walked over to her desk and hurriedly scribbled a note for the constable on duty informing him about the intruder at the gamekeeper's cottage. Her fingers were still numb from the cold and she had trouble keeping the fountain pen steady and her writing legible. She also drew the markings on the sole, as best as could recall from her memory, of the boot print left on the snow by the intruder. The note written, she blotted and then folded it, and asked Betsy to deliver it to Hobbs.

'Please make sure that you hand it over to the butler yourself. It is important that he passes this note on to the constable on duty as soon as possible.'

'I will, miss,' she said as she took the note and left the room.

Her duty done, Rachel walked over and sat in the armchair near the fireplace and allowed the comfort and warmth of the room, to thaw her out. Just as she could feel her fingers and toes once more, Jeremy walked in.

'I say, you are a sight for sore eyes. I was worried sick. I just got back from the village and met the housekeeper, Mrs. what's-her-name coming up the stairs. She told me you were still out in this ghastly weather.'

Rachel smiled, 'You mean Mrs. Simmons and yes I was. I just got back from Hogan's cottage. Did you manage to send the telegrams?'

Jeremy nodded, 'Just in time. Let's hope that they receive it. I'll bet the telegraph wires will be the first things to go if this weather continues. It's a miracle the telephone lines are still working. The roads will probably be closed soon.'

'What about the Countess and the others? Don't tell me they are going to be stranded.'

Jeremy responded, 'No, they are back already. I met Adam downstairs. Apparently, the hospital is just five miles away and they made good time despite the snow. Not much traffic on the roads. What about you? Did you find anything useful at the cottage?'

Rachel proceeded to tell him about her adventure du jour - her encounter with the unknown intruder and

Neville Pelham. Just as she reached the end of her story, they heard the clang of the lunch gong.

Ten minutes later, as they made their way to the dining room they saw Roderick wheeling in Lord Braybourne in his wheelchair.

Rachel greeted them, 'How nice to see you back, Lord Braybourne! How are you feeling?'

'Fit as a fiddle! If only everyone would stop fussing so much. I despise this confounded wheelchair,' he said grumpily.

Roderick spoke, 'Now now, Father, you know perfectly well that Dr. Farnsworth insisted on using it for a few days. He did say you were likely to be woozy.'

'Confounded doctors. What do they know? I tell you those emetics did the trick. Turns out I have the constitution of an ox. It will take more than a thimble full of poison to get me out of the way!'

Rachel laughed, 'Glad to hear it! And how is the other patient faring?'

Roderick replied, 'Much better, so we're told. Lord Marbury is still in a coma but they've removed the oxygen mask as all his vital functions are improving steadily. He is able to breathe on his own now. Although until he regains consciousness, he will remain on the I.V.'

Lord Braybourne spoke, 'That reminds me, I'm famished. I was on the blasted I.V. myself till this morning. A good square meal is what I need. Wheel on, boy!'

II

Post lunch, Jeremy decided to spend some time in the Hall's library, which according to him was the warmest place in the house, and asked Rachel if she wanted to join him. Rachel declined his offer and said she wanted to take a closer look at the photographs in the tin, which she had found hidden in Summer's room. They parted ways and after she retrieved the tin from her coat pocket, she went up to her room and sat on the rug in front of the fireplace, spreading out the five post card sized photographs in front of her.

The edges were yellow with time and the captions on the back informed her that were all taken between 1914 and 1924. Some were evidently shot in what looked like an English fishing village. There was a picture of an unsmiling man with a beret standing in front of a fishing trawler. The back had just one word written – 'Dad'.

There was a grainy family picture taken in a studio, where the same grim faced Dad in an army uniform was seated next to a blousy woman in a ditsy print dress – presumably Mum, who had a toddler on her lap and five children standing around the couple staring at the camera. Rachel noticed that the three boys in their knickerbockers looked as though they were in their mid-teens while the two young girls, one blonde and the other a brunette, looked younger, about twelve or thirteen years old. Turning the picture over, Rachel read the caption – The Marsh family and Ann Gibson, 1914. Rachel assumed the family picture was taken just before "Dad" went to fight the war.

Along with the photographs there was also a folded piece of paper. Upon unfolding it, she saw that it was a twenty five year old flyer dated 1924, which had a theatrical listing from Sadler's Wells in London. Probably a memento from a musical the Marsh family had attended. It was coming apart at the folds, possibly from age or from being folded and unfolded over the years.

The next picture that caught her eye was one, where the two girls now in their early twenties, were standing holding hands and smiling at the camera. The background was a fair of some sort and both young girls looked fresh and beautiful in their summer frocks and heels. Their hair was curled and they had the unfettered prettiness of the first flush of womanhood. Rachel turned the picture over to see their names scrawled behind – Libby Marsh & Ann Gibson 1924 at the Brixham Fair.

There were more pictures of the boys now grown up, standing in front of a similar fishing trawler. The caption at the back read, Ned, Toby and Peter Marsh, 1924. They had grown into handsome and strapping young lads. There was something about the boy in the middle, presumably Toby Marsh that made her take a second look. It was his smile. There was something uncannily familiar about his smile but she couldn't put her finger on where or on whom she had seen that smile. It bothered her. She knew she would keep thinking about it until she found out who it was but she also knew from experience that it would probably come to her like a bolt from the blue after she took her mind off it.

She put the picture back in the box and put her attention on the last remaining photograph. She reversed it to check the date and notice that it was taken right after the first war ended in 1918, the caption read 'Corporal Gibson & Private Marsh'. Turning it back, she gazed at the two men in uniform. Rachel realised that Private Marsh was the Dad from the family picture and further scrutiny of the second man, presumably Corporal Gibson revealed that he had a Victoria Cross pinned on his uniform.

Something nudged her to find out more about the Gibson family and why Ann Gibson was part of the Marsh family photographs. To Rachel's mind it seemed almost as though Ann had been adopted by the Marsh family during the war years. She made a note of names and dates and decided to request Chief Inspector Harrow to see if he could get more information from the War Office regarding Corporal Gibson and his daughter Ann.

The pictures seemed innocent enough. Which made Rachel wonder why Summer had hidden them. Hogan had mentioned that Summer was Libby's friend's child. In that case was Ann Gibson Summer's real mother? Even if it had no bearing on this case Rachel was consumed with curiosity to find out more. She was sure there was a connection somewhere between Summer and Ann Gibson. Was it possible that the pictures had something to do with Summer's murder?

She was lost in thought and came out of her reverie only when there was a knock on the door and Betsy entered bearing the news that there was a telephone call from Scotland Yard and that Jeremy had requested her to come down.

III

Rachel ran down the stairs to find Jeremy at the hall telephone. Jeremy beckoned her to listen into the earpiece. She heard him say, 'Are you quite sure, Chief Inspector, it wasn't just a relapse of some sort?'

Harrow's voice boomed from the other end, 'Of course I am sure! I have it on the best authority. Apart from the puncture wound made by the hypodermic needle, the constable on duty said that he went to answer nature's call and he was only away for about five minutes and when he got back, he saw a nurse come out from Lord Marbury's room. At the time he thought it was perfectly ordinary but later he was told that all the nurses were in the emergency ward and the surgery. Thanks to the snowstorm there were two nasty motor accidents and several people were brought in with critical injuries. So the nurses could not have been in the ward at the same time. And now he tells me that Lord Marbury's family was visiting around about the same time.'

'Yes the family did visit him but they came back quite cheerful with the news that Lord Marbury was well on the road to recovery!'

'He'll be lucky if he survives the night. A second murder attempt and right under our noses. The doctor thinks he was injected with a heavy dose of Morphine right about the time the family visited. He said he discovered the symptoms an hour later when the morphine began to kick in. Pupils constricted and all that. And now the poor man can't breathe without the aid of a breathing apparatus. If Lord Marbury dies on my watch, I'll have a lot to answer for, especially if I don't start making any arrests soon. A fine state of affairs, and to add insult to injury, I'm stuck in London and all the bloody roads are closed...'

'Look on the bright side Chief, at least the telephone lines are up! Hello! Hello!' Jeremy shouted back tapping the metal cradle. But it was no good. The telephone line had just gone dead.

Rachel raised her eyebrow, 'Looks like you spoke too soon, Jeremy. I'm afraid you're developing a black tongue. Now don't you go and say anything about the electric lights.'

'Oh, I wouldn't worry about the lights if I were you. Unless the fuse box is open to the elements, which I don't suppose it...oh!'

Before he could finish, the lights flickered and they were engulfed in darkness.

'Jeremy!'

'I suppose that was my fault as well?' Jeremy asked tongue-in-cheek.

'If this goes on, we'll have to seriously think of trading in the car for a broomstick,' Rachel chirped back.

'I don't mind in the least bit. Imagine the money we'll save on petrol.'

'Hush. I can hear someone coming,' Rachel said as the hall was suddenly filled with voices murmuring and the baize door opened to a flickering of candle light.

The servants walked in single file holding aloft lit candle stands. Hobbs and Mrs. Simmons were supervising the ritual. One by one each room on the ground floor was lit by the bevy of footmen, while one file of maids went up the stairs under Mrs. Simmons' command and Rachel had no doubt that the first floor would be taken care of with similar military precision.

Chapter Eighteen

The family had gathered in the library upon Jeremy's request. The large fireplace provided a good deal of warmth and ample candles provided enough light to see by. He had particularly wanted to break the news first to all those who had been involved in the hospital visit.

As they made themselves comfortable the Countess asked, 'What is it? Has something happened?'

Jeremy nodded. 'I'm afraid I must be the bearer of bad tidings. I, rather we, that is my wife and I had a telephone call a few minutes ago from Chief Inspector Harrow of Scotland Yard. As he himself cannot personally be here to take part in the investigation, owing to the fact that the roads are currently inaccessible, it is my unpleasant task to inform you that a second murder attempt was made on Lord Marbury's life earlier today.'

The Countess paled, 'Oh my God! But he was so much better. Another murder attempt? What does that mean? Is he...?'

'As of now, he is alive but barely so. The doctor is doing everything he can but it would not be wise on my part if I didn't tell you that Lord Marbury is in a critical state as we speak. He may not survive the night.'

Miranda who was sitting next to the Countess took her hand and addressing Stephanie she said, 'Darling Stephanie, get your mother some brandy, would you?' She then turned to Jeremy, 'But he is alive? And that means there is a fighting chance and if I know anything about Magnus, it's this – he is a fighter.'

Lady Claire spoke calmly, 'Tell me, how was my father attacked this time?'

Rachel spoke, 'We believe that he was injected with a large dose of morphine. They found a puncture wound made by a hypodermic syringe and the doctor claims that he exhibited all the classic symptoms of a morphine overdose an hour after you all visited.'

Lady Stephanie spoke up as she handed a brandy snifter to her mother, 'Which means that someone tried to murder him just an hour after we left? How awful.'

Miranda shook her head, 'No darling, it means someone injected him while we were visiting. Morphine takes a while to act, which means it could have been any one of us, isn't that right, Mr. Richards?'

Jeremy nodded, 'I'm afraid we cannot rule out that possibility.'

Lady Claire lost her usual air of cool calm assurance and looked panic stricken, 'What are you all saying? That one of us... oh, God! This can't be happening. This is a nightmare!'

Miranda spoke, 'I think we could all use a brandy. Stephanie, do call Hobbs!'

Jeremy cleared his throat, 'No, Lady Stephanie, I'd rather you didn't. Not just yet. You see, I need to ask you all some questions and I would prefer a certain level of privacy...'

Miranda nodded, 'Of course, how silly of me. Please carry on. You could start with me if you like.'

'Thank you. I need to know everything about your hospital visit starting from the time you all entered the premises.'

Miranda responded, 'Yes, of course. Catherine was the first person to go in and visit Magnus. She sat with him for about fifteen minutes and came out. Claire went in next. She was in his room for just five minutes...'

Lady Claire spoke up, 'Yes that's right. You see, I can't bear to see Papa like that. And I've always hated hospitals. I just...'

The Countess spoke gently, 'It's alright, darling. We all know how much you dote on your Papa.'

Rachel spoke, 'I've been meaning to ask, did you see the constable on duty?'

The Countess responded, 'Why, yes. He was there sitting on a chair outside the door when I went to see Magnus.'

'And where were all the others? Were they out in the hallway?'

Lady Claire spoke, 'No, I think Stephanie and Aunt Miranda went to get themselves some coffee while I waited in the reception area with Adam.'

Jeremy asked, 'Then what happened?

'Mama came out and told me I could go in and I did but I didn't see the constable outside the door or anyone else for that matter. There is a nurse's station just two doors before my father's room and I walked past it and there was no one there either. I remember thinking it quite odd at the time. Almost eerie as though the hospital was deserted. The long corridor with all doors shut on either side and not a soul in sight.'

Jeremy nodded, 'I see. Can you think of anything else that struck you as odd?'

'Yes as I was leaving, I crossed the nurse's station and I heard the sound of footsteps so I looked back and there was a nurse approaching me but when I smiled at her, she just turned her back on me and walked away in the opposite direction. I thought it rather rude at the time.'

'Can you remember what this nurse looked like?'

'Now that you mention it, there was something odd about her, well apart from her behaviour. She had very thick brows – like a man's and thick ankles and she was rather heavy set.'

'What did you do after that?'

'Umm, yes. I came back to the reception area and as Miranda and Stephanie had not returned, I asked Adam if he wanted his turn and he said yes. So I sat besides Mama and gave her company while he went in.'

'I think we had better ask Adam to join us. It is imperative for us to know what he saw or if he spotted the nurse as well.'

'The nurse? You don't think that she was...?'

Jeremy cut in. 'There is something very sinister about this nurse. You see, the constable on duty reported that when he came back on duty he saw a nurse leave your father's room and as all the nurses were called away on a sudden emergency duty, it could only mean that the nurse you saw wasn't a real nurse.'

Lady Claire spoke, 'I'll go and call Adam right away.'

Miranda suddenly stood up. 'No. let me. It will seem more natural if I wanted his company. That Ada creature will probably be stuck to him like a barnacle and is bound to ask a hundred questions if you go,' she said and walked out of the room.

While Miranda was gone, Rachel asked, 'Did any of you visit Lord Braybourne while you were there?'

Lady Stephanie answered, 'Well, yes. Miranda and I looked into his room when we went to get coffee but he wasn't there.'

Jeremy looked up suddenly, 'What do you mean he wasn't there?'

Lady Stephanie shrugged, 'I mean exactly what I said. He wasn't in his room.'

Rachel looked puzzled, 'But I thought you brought him back with you.'

Lady Stephanie clarified, 'No, I believe he was discharged after we left. He came back later with Ada in his own car. We didn't have room in ours for him and the wheelchair.'

Rachel spoke, 'I see. So you didn't meet him at all?'

Lady Claire answered, 'I don't know about the others but I certainly didn't want to spend any more time in that hospital.'

The Countess also responded, 'I'm afraid, I didn't either.'

Just then the library door opened and Miranda returned with Adam in tow. She prodded him and said, 'Tell Mr. Richards what you just told me.'

Adam spoke, 'I did cross a nurse as I was walking towards Lord Marbury's room and at the time I confess I thought rather uncharitable thoughts.'

'Uncharitable or not, I think you had better share them,' Miranda quipped.

'Well, the first thought that crossed my mind was that if I were being attended to by a nurse like that, even if I were in a coma, I'd probably get well in record time and run for the hills. She reminded me of those men you see in pantomimes wearing bright red lipstick and a lady's dress.'

Jeremy looked amused and said, 'Thank you. That is most helpful. By the way did you see the constable on duty?'

Adam furrowed his brows, 'Yes. He had just returned to his post, I think.'

'I see and how long were you with Lord Marbury?'

'About two or three minutes when Lady Stephanie knocked and came in. I left her and went back and joined the others.'

'Did you notice any wound on him? Like a puncture mark made by a syringe.'

Adam replied, 'No, I'm sorry I didn't go close enough. I'm afraid I sat on the visitor's chair near the door and just chatted with him. That is, I told him about the weather and how everyone was missing him awfully and so on.'

Lady Stephanie smiled, 'Yes, I heard you talking before I knocked. I thought it was rather sweet.'

'And how long were you in your father's room, Lady Stephanie?'

'Not very long, I think. When Adam vacated the chair and left, I sat in it for a while looking at Papa wondering about what was going on in his head, if he was even aware of his surroundings or just in a state of limbo and I don't know how long I just sat there thinking how we used to go riding across the estate every Tuesday and how kind he was with everyone and who would do something like this to him and ...' Stephanie broke down.

The Countess got up and went to her, 'Come my darling, you must be strong for your Papa's sake. Let's go to your room. Would you excuse us, Mr. Richards? If there is anything else you would like to ask Stephanie or me...'

'No. Please go ahead. I am so sorry,' Jeremy said softly as he walked ahead and held the door open for mother and daughter.

Miranda spoke after Jeremy closed the door behind them. 'Looks like I am the last one left to question. Stephanie was in there for ages so Catherine asked me to go and check on her and I did. The child was just sitting on that chair quietly staring at her father with tears streaming down her face. I couldn't bear it. So I just wiped her tears and told Magnus that I'd visit him another day and we left. And before you ask, yes I did see the constable on duty and no, I did not see the pantomime nurse. Now if we're done here, I'd really like to join my sister and my niece.'

Jeremy nodded and as the others left, he held Rachel back by the wrist and whispered in her ears, 'I think it's time we had a chat with Lord Braybourne, don't you?'

'Well, darling it's like you've become a mind reader as well. What colour would you prefer your broomstick to be?'

'I've always been rather partial to grey', Jeremy deadpanned.

Chapter Nineteen

As Jeremy and Rachel left the library, they heard a commotion in the hall. Voices were raised and they could hear a woman's voice shout, 'Let me go, you brute! I haven't done anything! You can't hold me without a charge.'

A gruff male voice shouted back, 'We'll see about that, won't we, luv? To begin with, I'm charging you with assaulting a police officer.'

More shouting ensued and as Jeremy and Rachel reached the hall and Jeremy asked the large uniformed figure, 'Constable, what is going on?' The constable looked up and Rachel noticed that he had bloody scratches on his face and a fast developing black eye. The young woman must have put up quite a fight, despite the fact that he was a head taller than her and twice her size.

The young constable touched his helmet, which was askew and responded, 'PC Downs at your service, Sir! I caught this young woman outside the gamekeeper's cottage attempting to bury this sack in the snow.' He held up a dirty brown cloth bag made from a sacking material before continuing, 'She then attempted to make a run for it when I asked her what she was doing. And then when I caught up with her, she kicked, scratched and punched me.' He imparted the last nugget of information with an indignant look bordering on astonishment.

The young woman in question was dressed like a tramp in baggy trousers and an old coat three sizes larger than her own. She was wearing brown gardening boots. Her dirty blonde hair was untied and fell about her face under the floppy brown gardening hat. Rachel could not see her face as her head was bowed under the hat. She looked defeated as though the fire had finally gone out of her.

By this time a bevy of staff and a few members of the household had gathered in the hall to see what the commotion was all about.

Rachel noticed that the girl's knuckles were bloody and said gently, 'I think she needs medical attention. You both do. What is your name, girl?'

The girl looked up teary eyed and Rachel gave a gasp, 'Goodness, Ivy! It's you! I think, PC Downs, you had better bring your charge in to the study. She has some explaining to do.' Then turning to the housekeeper, she said, 'Mrs. Simmons could you please send in some hot water, iodine and cotton wool?'

They moved in to the study and Rachel told Hobbs that they were not to be disturbed and closed the door behind her.

The constable asked with some bewilderment, 'You know this girl, milady?'

Rachel ignored the milady title and answered, 'We certainly do. She's the same housemaid that was reported missing twenty four hours ago. Her name is Ivy. She's been hiding in the gamekeeper's cottage. She ran when I visited there this morning.' Then turning to Ivy she said, 'It was you up in the attic, wasn't it?'

Ivy looked down at her boots and said nothing.

Rachel continued, 'I believe, PC Downs, if you look at the soles of her shoes they will be consistent with the markings of the intruder which I found in the snow outside the gamekeeper's cottage. The one I drew in the note I sent you.'

Jeremy spoke up. 'Well, what have you to say for yourself, Ivy?'

Ivy answered plaintively, 'I didn't do it, Sir!'

Jeremy asked, 'Didn't do what exactly, Ivy?'

'I didn't murder anyone. I just found it stuffed in the cupboard and then when I heard about Lord Braybourne being poisoned, I knew they'd hang me but I swear, I didn't do it!'

Jeremy shook his head, 'You're not making any sense. Slow down. Now let's start at the beginning.'

'I didn't do it! I swear I didn't do it,' she repeated like a stuck record.

Rachel emptied the cloth sack on the study table and a heap of black and white clothing that looked like a maid's uniform tumbled out. A brown glass bottle rolled out alongside as Rachel held up a bloodstained white lace apron. 'I think, Jeremy, she is referring to Summer's murder and the Baron's poisoning. There's blood on this maid's uniform and I think what we have here, is the missing vial of belladonna concentrate.'

The constable spoke. 'What is your full name, girl?'

'It's Ivy Roberts,' she mumbled back.

'Well Ivy Roberts, you're nicked alright. I am charging you with the murder of the maid, Summer Hogan and the attempted murder of Lord Braybourne apart from grievous bodily assault on a police constable. You do not have to say anything if you do not wish to do so, but anything you do say may be used against you in a court of law...'

'Please madam, help me! Don't let 'em hang me for something I didn't do. I know if anyone can help me, it'll be you.'

Rachel asked, 'Then why did you run when you knew it was me at the cottage and why were you trying to hide the evidence?'

Ivy replied round eyed, 'I wasn't sure you would believe me.'

Rachel said, 'If you are innocent as you claim, I would have been more inclined to believe you, had you at least made an attempt to come down from the attic and explain how you came to find this bloodstained uniform and this bottle.'

'It's my spare apron! It was stuffed in my cupboard! Who would believe me if I told them that I had no idea how I got blood on it or how the bottle came to be empty!'

Rachel looked at her contemplatively and asked, 'Where on earth did you get the extraordinary clothes you are wearing?'

Ivy said sheepishly, 'They were in a box of old clothes in the attic. It was freezing up there and I looked for something warmer than what I had on. Besides, my things were wet and I had torn the coat and the uniform I was wearing while climbing up the ivy. It was so cold, I thought I would die.'

Rachel nodded, 'You are brave, I'll grant you that but...'

'I swear, madam, please believe me, I didn't kill anyone.'

PC Downs huffed, 'You can swear all you like, but I know a violent criminal when I see one, oh yes, I do. You, Missy, are going into lockup as soon as the roads open again. Meanwhile...'

Before he could finish, Mrs. Simmons came in with a tray containing the items Rachel had asked her to bring in. She laid down the tray and asked Rachel, 'Is there anything else I can get you, madam?'

'No, thank you, Mrs. Simmons but you could help us with something. We need a safe place preferably without windows to hold Ivy for the night. Given her penchant for running away, a strong lockable door would be preferable as well! Hopefully by tomorrow the roads will be open and Constable Downs will arrange for her transfer to the local police station but till such time we must make sure she doesn't run away again, for our peace of mind, not to mention her own safety.'

Mrs. Simmons said, 'Well, madam, there is the old meat locker next to the pantry downstairs that has a sturdy door and no windows. It's quite empty. Ever since our refrigeration unit came in, we have no more use for it. '

'Are you sure, Mrs. Simmons? We don't want her freezing to death!'

'I'll have a spare bed put in there and give the girl extra blankets and a hot water bottle. I'm sure she will be quite alright.'

Rachel spoke, 'Thank you Mrs. Simmons. I suppose if Ivy could survive a night in Mr. Hogan's freezing attic, she will be quite alright here. Now let's clean up those wounds, shall we?'

Chapter Twenty

Half an hour later the dinner gong went off. Rachel who had finished playing nurse to Ivy and the constable had just enough time left over to freshen up upstairs but not enough to change into formals. She hoped that the others would overlook her tardiness as she made her way to the dining room.

The lavish dining room looked even more splendid tonight as hordes of candles flickered in their ornate candle-stands throwing an ochre glow on the sombre old masters on the walls. Their flickering light glinted to and fro, from the bevelled crystal droplets on the chandeliers to the shining silverware and cut glass goblets on the table.

Rachel realised she was the last person in. She entered without ceremony and took her seat beside Miranda before apologising to all. 'I am so sorry I didn't have time to dress for dinner. I hope you will forgive me.'

Miranda spoke, 'Nobody minds, my dear. Not these days. I don't know why we bother to deck up night after night anyway. It's such an archaic old custom that ought to have died along with our Victorian ancestors.'

Lady Claire spoke in her precise manner, 'I don't know, Aunt Miranda; I quite like it. I think it is the one custom that keeps us civilised and differentiates us from the barbarians.'

Miranda laughed, 'My dear if dressing for dinner was the only hallmark of civilised people, our civilisation would have a lot to answer for.'

Ada Cellini who was beautifully dressed in another one of her fine gowns spoke up with disdain, 'Oh you English, you make me laugh! Who cares about your silly ideals? All this pomp and show, eh and Britannia rules the world. What is this civilisation you speak of? All you have done is you have looted and robbed and enslaved so many countries, stolen people's lives and their nation's treasures like robber barons and you call yourselves civilised because you dress for dinner, ha!'

'Mother, please!' Andrew beseeched as Ada flashed her eyes at him.

The Countess spoke up in her vague way, 'I daresay Ada, you could be right but I do think this kind of talk at dinner is likely to give one indigestion, don't you?'

Baron Braybourne cut in. 'And I can give you all a first-hand account of what that's like! Agony! I'd much rather do justice to Mrs. Meade's fine cooking for now and advise all the beautiful women here to leave debates over colonialism to the Parliament!'

Ada laughed, 'Oh, you are a funny man. You want us women to be, how you say, like the chickens with our heads in the sand.'

Andrew gave an amused laugh and said, 'She means ostrich, don't you, Mother?'

Ada flashed back, 'It is amusing for my son to correct everything I say. Such a British habit, no? Ooh la la, somebody got a silly word wrong! It is so amusing for you all, is it not?'

Adam who had stayed quiet through the conversation spoke up between mouthfuls, 'What is even more amusing, is how you all are doing your darndest to completely ignore the elephant in the room.'

Ada shrugged. 'All this talk of animals, it is so confusing.'

Roderick spoke, 'I am sorry, am I missing something here? Which elephant are you referring to?'

Adam answered with his gaze on Rachel and then Jeremy, 'The elephant that was found and charged with murder tonight. The one that is hopefully being locked up somewhere in the house as we speak.'

Jeremy cleared his throat, 'I'm afraid she may have been found with some incriminating evidence but ...'

Ada cut in, 'What? Who? Nobody tells me anything!'

Andrew responded, 'That may be because you are apt to make such a song and dance about things, Mother. Please can we discuss this later?'

Ada dropped her fork. 'No! Who has been caught? Who is this "she" you speak of?'

The Countess spoke, 'Oh, Ada, I agree with Andrew. I don't think we should be discussing this at the table.'

Miranda challenged her, 'Why not, Catherine? Now that Adam has let the proverbial elephant out of the bag so to speak; I'm sure you can see that we're all agog with curiosity.'

The Countess sighed, 'Well, alright. Rachel, you can tell them, I suppose.'

Rachel responded, 'Why not, since some of you know already. For those who don't; it was one of the maids – Ivy. The one who went missing yesterday. The constable arrested her a while ago as she was trying to bury some evidence in the woods, which included bloodstained clothes and the empty vial of Madame Cellini's belladonna concentrate.'

'Well I'll be dashed, that little chit of a girl! Did she say why she tried to poison me?' Lord Braybourne enquired.

Rachel answered, 'No. That's just it, you see. She denies it. She says she panicked when she found those things in her cupboard but has no idea how they got there.'

Ada looked at her unbelievingly, 'Of course she would! What sort of detectives are you anyway?'

Rachel sighed, 'The kind that gives a person the benefit of doubt, I'm afraid. There is a small possibility that those things could have just as easily been planted in the girl's cupboard. If you ask me I think the girl may have been framed.'

Lord Braybourne asked, 'And where is this girl now?'

Rachel answered him with a cryptic smile, 'I'm afraid that is top secret. Suffice to say she's in a safe place for the night. And she is well-guarded. After all, if she was framed, we wouldn't the real killer to get to her tonight, would we?'

II

After dinner, Miranda, Adam, Neville and the Countess sat down to a game of bridge in the sitting room while Roderick put a record on the gramophone. As a soft waltz played he asked Lady Stephanie for a dance. She shook her head and Rachel heard him say, 'Come on, Steph, I daresay it will take your mind off things.'

Lady Stephanie smiled wanly and got up to join him. Andrew and Lady Claire joined in the dancing after a while. Ada excused herself to go and powder her nose. Jeremy and Rachel took the opportunity to quietly invite the Baron to join them for a post prandial nightcap in the study. He agreed with alacrity and Jeremy wheeled him into the adjoining study where the fire was burning brightly.

Once the door was shut, the music became faint and the Baron said, 'This is a relief. All this music and dancing gives me a headache these days. I must be getting old.'

Rachel said, 'Nonsense, Lord Braybourne. You are probably just exhausted from your exertions at the hospital.'

'The only thing I had to exert was my voice from time to time. I found the young nurses to be quite incompetent. Nothing like they used to be in the old days. Can't even give one a sponge bath properly. Nursing standards have definitely dropped.'

'Interesting you should say that,' Rachel said with a smile.

Jeremy gave her a look and said to the Baron, 'I'm afraid there is no port here. Can I interest you in a brandy or would you like me to ring for some port.'

'Brandy will do, just as long as it's not poisoned this time, mind!' The Baron quipped as Jeremy filled three glasses.

Jeremy smiled as he handed him a glass and said, 'Plenty of good faith. Even so, I'll have the first sip just to make sure it isn't. Cheers.'

Rachel sat in an armchair next to the Baron's wheelchair and asked casually, 'So Lord Braybourne, how did you find your old friend, Lord Marbury when you visited him this morning?'

'He was just fine. I... er... who told you I visited him this morning?'

'Just a guess. Given that your room was just a few doors away from him, wasn't it?'

'No it wasn't. My room was on the other end, near the emergency ward.'

'Did you walk down or use your wheelchair?' She asked.

'Of course I didn't use my wheelchair. I didn't have a wheelchair then. I say, what are you getting at?'

'Nothing. It's just that when Miranda and Lady Stephanie looked in on you this morning, they said they didn't find you in your room and yet the funny thing is, they didn't see a wheelchair either.'

'What time did they say they looked in?'

'Sometime during the visiting hours between nine and ten.'

'Ah! That explains it! You see, sometime before nine they told me I was to be discharged this morning and I asked if I could get out and about, anything to be out of the poky little dump of a room they had put me in. So, the nurse wheeled me in to this place they call the recuperating room a little after nine. They have a wireless set installed there, probably to distract and amuse all the old fogies who give them too much trouble. And she didn't come back for me till quarter past ten. Apparently she got caught up in some emergency. Balderdash! If you ask me, they're just downright incompetent these days.'

Rachel was puzzled. 'So when did you visit Lord Marbury?'

'Right after they took off the I.V. At about eight in the morning, I think. No one told me I couldn't walk, up until then, so when the nurse skedaddled I sneaked out to see how Magnus was getting along. I spent ten minutes with him and then got back to my room. Just in time too. A few minutes later they brought in this blasted wheelchair and told me I was to be discharged in an hour or so from that miserable place. But why are you asking me all these questions?'

Jeremy answered, 'We thought you knew. A second murder attempt was made on Lord Marbury's life today, sometime between nine and ten this morning.'

'And you think I had something to do with it?'

Jeremy shrugged. 'Well, at this point, it's just procedure. We've got to know the whereabouts of anyone who was in the hospital around that time.'

'I see.'

Rachel spoke, 'Tell me, Lord Braybourne were there other patients there who can vouch for the fact you stayed in the recuperating room between nine and ten this morning?'

'Of course there were. At least five or six decrepit old sods but God only knows if they can vouch for anything. They all seemed to be in varying stages of decay.'

'So you can't remember anyone in particular?'

'Wait. There was this one chap, some old Major something-or-the-other, who seemed alright up until he started boring me to death with tales about his regimental days in India. I don't know much else about him but his memory certainly seemed to be alright. Painfully so. Perhaps you could ask him.'

'Thank you, we will.'

'Now if that's all, do you mind wheeling me back to the sitting room? I don't seem to have mastered the art of navigating myself in this thing quite as yet. Also I seem to have finished my designated quota of brandy. I think I'll oust young Pelham and take over for the next hand of bridge.'

Jeremy answered, 'Certainly. Tell me, if you are quite comfortable walking about by yourself, why the wheelchair?'

'I like the attention,' Lord Braybourne gave a small laugh before continuing. 'No, really, at first I didn't like the idea at all. I was quite sure I would stop using it as soon as we got back to the Hall but later, I began thinking that it wouldn't hurt if I used it for a day or two, out of a misplaced sense of curiosity, I suppose. I wondered what it must feel like for those chaps who were wounded in the war.'

Rachel raised an eyebrow, 'Like an experiment, you mean?'

'Quite.'

'And what have you discovered?' Rachel asked.

Lord Braybourne answered as Jeremy began wheeling him towards the door, 'I don't mind it as much as I thought I would. In fact it is like riding about in a small personal car. Perhaps, one day they'll invent something similar for busy office goers who have the use of their limbs and still prefer to ride about on a set of wheels within large buildings.'

'Interesting thought,' Jeremy said as Rachel held the door open for them.

He continued, 'However, I think the human mind is an exceptional tool. You see, if I were told that I had lost the use of my legs, I probably would have hated it. But as long as I know that I can get up and stretch my legs and walk about whenever I like, it's not so bad after all.'

After Jeremy and Rachel had deposited Lord Braybourne back to the sitting room, they noticed that the two couples were still waltzing. Jeremy smiled and asked Rachel for a dance. As they began to waltz, he whispered in her ears, 'That's one theory blown out of the window. If it wasn't the Baron, who was it?'

Rachel whispered back as she twirled, 'I don't know, darling. It could've been anyone who can't be accounted for. Even Hogan wasn't at the cottage but then I can't even begin to imagine him in a nurse's uniform, can you?'

'No darling, besides I don't think the nurse had a large bushy moustache or someone would have mentioned it,' Jeremy grinned.

'Oh, I can't think anymore. My mind is in complete disarray. I'm beginning to feel a bit like Alice in Wonderland.'

Jeremy looked as though he was concerned for her mental health. 'Are you quite alright, darling?'

Rachel put his mind at rest by saying, 'Of course I am. It's just that this case seems to be getting curiouser and curiouser. Like we're still falling down the rabbit hole with no end in sight!'

Chapter Twenty One

The next morning, Rachel could not shrug off the nagging feeling that she had missed asking Ivy something important. She finally realised what it was as soon as Neville Pelham joined her at the breakfast table.

Rachel rushed through the remainder of her breakfast and excused herself from the table to go downstairs and meet Ivy. As soon as Rachel entered the servant's hall, chairs were pushed back from the table as all the servants rose as a sign of courtesy towards her. Mrs. Simmons gave her a welcoming smile and Hobbs the butler greeted her graciously. Apart from Betsy, a few of the other staff members smiled at her too. Rachel was pleasantly surprised since she had received a rather frosty reception on all her prior visits behind the baize door. It made her wonder what she owed her good press to.

She greeted Mr. Hobbs and Mrs. Simmons and smiled at the others, 'Oh, please don't let me interrupt your breakfast. I just wanted a word with Ivy, if that's alright.' Her eyes came to rest on Ivy, who had evidently been set free by Mrs. Simmons and was having her breakfast with the others under the constable's watchful gaze. The girl looked refreshingly different this morning in a clean black dress with her hair neatly tied back in a bun. She glanced at Mrs. Simmons who nodded encouragingly at her while PC Downs frowned and said, 'I don't think I should allow that till the inspector gets here. Now that the fugitive is under arrest, it's against procedure.'

Mrs. Simmons spoke up, 'Oh, stuff and nonsense. It's only Ivy. You needn't be so officious about it. Besides with all the roads closed, it could take ages for the inspector to get here.'

PC Downs spoke with authority, 'I'm sorry but the law is the law. As it is I've let you bully me into allowing her out for breakfast and er...other things. And she's going right back to the lockup after this.'

Mrs. Simmons said, 'What lockup? That's my meat locker!'

Her outburst made him more determined. He spoke with his nose in the air, 'That is as may be. I am sorry, I cannot give her any more allowances till the inspector gets here. The law is the law.'

Rachel had not expected this response and decided to bluff her way through. She spoke with an air of polite confidence, 'Thank you, Constable but I am quite aware of police procedure given that my husband was with the Scotland Yard and you may not be aware but Chief Inspector Harrow himself has given us complete authority to investigate. It is perfectly alright if I question her. Now, if you would step this way, Ivy.'

As Ivy came to her side, the constable was left with no choice but to open and shut his mouth like a goldfish.

Mrs. Simmons led the way to the butler's pantry and after ushering them in, she shut the door behind them. PC Downs was left standing in the hallway. She gave him a cold stare and walked away.

Rachel sat in a chair and spoke, 'Now Ivy, while you were up in Mr. Hogan's attic, going through boxes, did you find any books or papers or letters? Think carefully, this is important.'

'No, I wasn't looking for books or papers, madam. Just something to keep me warm.'

'Yes, of course I know that but you must have gone through the place before you found those clothes. There must have been other boxes.'

'Oh, yes, there were a few other boxes and trunks but they had things like gardening tools and such like. I found a box full of broken candle stands and parts of old paraffin lamps – things like that but I don't recall any books or papers. Oh, yes! There was a pile of old newspapers tied up in strings probably kept to be used as spills for the fireplace or something else later.'

'No, not newspapers. You see, Ivy, a bundle of letters that were written to Summer have disappeared and we did search the rest of the house without any success. The only place we didn't look in, was the attic because you had moved something over the trapdoor and we couldn't get access. What was is by the way?'

She answered sheepishly. 'An old tin trunk full of tools. It was the heaviest thing up there that I could move.'

'I see.'

'But madam, did you say you were searching for letters? Written to Summer?'

'Yes. Why?'

'It just seems odd that's all.'

'Why do you say that?'

'Because she couldn't read very well. We used to make fun of her by making her read out things. She left school early and never learned how to read proper like. Anyone who knew her would've known that.'

'I see. That is odd. Do you mean to tell me that she could not read at all?'

'She had difficulty reading labels. Just last month Mrs. Meade got terribly upset when she asked her to fetch a box of baking soda from the pantry and Summer brought her a box of soap powder instead. Mrs. Meade didn't notice at first as she had a lot of work that day. All the kitchen maids had been awful busy too. They had to send up five courses for two dozen dinner guests. It was His Lordship's birthday and when the cake was sent down cut but uneaten, she tasted it and realised what had happened. I remember because the rest of us laughed about it and chaffed her for days after that. I feel sorry about it now. Poor Summer – Mrs. Meade gave her hell alright; she was that upset.'

Rachel's eyes were far off as her mind digested this new bit of information. It dawned on her that Neville had lied about what he had been searching for in Hogan's cottage. She said, 'Thank you, Ivy. You have no idea just how helpful you've been.'

'I am so glad, madam. I'll do anything to help you. All of us would. James – the footman, who was in the dining room last night told me and the others this morning how you stood up for me when everyone else at dinner, especially that foreign lady was ready to send me to the gallows. And I am ashamed now that I didn't come to you sooner for help when I could. I am sorry that I thought you wouldn't believe me.'

'Oh, Ivy! All I said was that there is a possibility that you could have been framed, that's all. But I do wish you had come to me earlier. It would've saved us all a lot of trouble. Anyway, there's no point in dwelling on that now. If you are innocent and now I am beginning to believe that could be the case, we have to find a way of getting you out of this mess.'

Ivy looked down at her shoes and said, 'Yes, madam. I am right sorry, madam.'

Rachel nodded, 'Well, sorry isn't going to solve this case. You could start by telling me exactly how and when you found the apron and the bottle of belladonna.'

'The same night after we found Summer lying dead in the linen room. Mrs. Simmons had asked me to take a dinner tray up for you. I realised that I had spilled something on my apron and went up to my room to get my spare apron. I couldn't find it at first and I was in a hurry so I started pulling out things from my wardrobe when I found it tucked behind some other clothes. Almost as if someone had tried to keep it hidden from me. If I hadn't pulled out the other clothes, I would have never seen it myself.'

'Go on.'

'I was scared of course and I knew the police would search our rooms so I hid the apron in the broom closet on the servant's floor along with some rags in a sack. And then I ran down to bring you the dinner tray. I swear I almost told you when you asked me if there was anything else I wanted to share but I was too scared.'

'Yes, now I do recall. You did look nervy that night. What about the brown bottle? When did you find that?'

'I found that the next evening right after I heard Lord Braybourne had been poisoned with belladonna. I rushed to the pantry where I remembered I had kept it after mixing the eye drop solution for that foreign lady. It was close to full the night before. When I found it, sure enough it was empty and I panicked. I knew they were likely to blame me for it seeing as she had given it to me. I took the empty bottle and then went up and got the apron from the broom closet and left the house without telling anyone. You know the rest, madam.'

'Yes I certainly do. By the way, what about that girl who rooms with you – Myrtle. Could she have hidden the apron in your cupboard?'

Ivy sounded hesitant, 'I suppose so, but no, madam. She would never put me in a fix like that. She's my friend!'

'Hmm.' Rachel's heart went out to the trusting young girl in front of her and she knew in that instant that she believed every single word Ivy had uttered.

Chapter
Twenty Two

Rachel went in search for Neville Pelham as soon as her interview with Ivy was over. She stopped in front of a window on the staircase landing. The light coming through it dazzled her eyes. Curiosity made her pause. Looking out she realised that the heavy clouds had parted to give way to brilliant sunshine, which reflected off the melting snow to produce a high degree of luminescence. She found herself thinking that it wouldn't be long before the roads open up again.

Turning back to the task at hand, she resumed walking and made her way through the main corridor. She stopped to ask a passing footman where she could find Mr. Pelham. He informed her that he had seen all the young gentlemen heading towards the billiards room.

She walked for a bit and as she neared, she followed the sound of balls being knocked about on the billiards table and discreetly entered the billiards room.

She found Neville leaning over the table with his cue while the others stood watching. His brow was furrowed and he had a serious look on his face. Once he started playing she realised why. One by one he began potting balls in succession while Roderick, Andrew and Adam looked on in admiration. When he finished, they clapped in unison, and spoke all at once.

'Good show, old boy!'

'Splendid!'

'You know, you could make money with a talent like that. You would put all the bookies out of business!'

Neville winced at the mention of bookies and shook his head back at them, 'I'd rather run a mile in tight shoes, thank you. I've had enough dealings with bookies to last me a lifetime. Oh, hello Rachel. Didn't know you were a witness to my little parlour game.'

Rachel responded, 'And I had no idea that you were such a wizard at billiards. Quite impressive, really.'

'That was snooker, my dear, not billiards.'

'I stand corrected. Whatever it was, you were rather brilliant at it!'

'One aims to please,' he said with a mock bow.

Rachel smiled. 'Glad to hear it, Mr. Pelham. If you are done here, might I steal you away? Something's come up and we need to talk.'

'That sounds ominous!'

'Oh, I should hope not. Shall we?' She said motioning towards the door.

They left the others to continue with the game and headed towards Lord Marbury's study.

Once they had made themselves comfortable in the armchairs near the fireplace, Neville offered her a cigarette from the cigarette box on the table. She accepted and he lit it for her before lighting his own.

Blowing out a smoke ring, he asked, 'So, how can I help you?'

'Well, I've just had a very interesting chat with Ivy.'

'Ah! The maid who was locked up yesterday?'

'Yes, and she had something strange to say, when I happened to ask her, if she had found any letters in Hogan's attic. You know, the ones you had supposedly written to Summer.'

'I say, you aren't helping, you know, by going about asking the staff about those letters. Kind of shoots down the very idea about trying to keep it under wraps, doesn't it?'

'Oh, don't be so stuffy. Of course I didn't tell her who they were supposedly from.'

'Oh, alright. That's not so bad then.'

'But it is, in a way. You see she looked puzzled and told me that the letters couldn't have been meant for Summer since she couldn't read.'

'What? The girl is talking rot. It's not like we're living in the dark ages. Of course she could read. Everybody can these days.'

'Not everybody apparently. Summer couldn't.' Rachel then proceeded to tell him the story about the mix up that Summer had made with the labels.

'That could be put down to a simple mistake. Now I'm not saying Summer was one of the Bronte sisters but it also doesn't prove that she couldn't read.'

'I'm a little more inclined to believe that she couldn't, purely judging from the fact that her lack of reading skills had become a standing joke in the servant's hall.'

Neville murmured, 'I see.'

'Do you?' Rachel asked with a raised eyebrow. 'Because if that be the case, I wonder what you were really searching for, in her room at the cottage?'

'What? I didn't know she couldn't read. How can you doubt my word based on some silly maid's talk?' He spluttered in disbelief.

Rachel shook her head. 'I think you've played your hand and lost this round already. No point in playing the same cards all over again.'

'I don't know what you mean.'

'Don't you? By all accounts, you're a betting man and surely even you can see that it would take a special kind of stupid to believe your "love letter" theory, after all of this. And I'm afraid I just don't fit the bill.'

'No, you are right. I am sorry. I don't know what to say.'

'I can help you there. The truth would be a perfectly good place to start as any.'

'Alright, but don't blame me if it sounds a lot more farfetched than my so called love letters.'

'Try me.'

'Some time ago, two weeks before someone took a shot at Magnus, Summer told me in confidence that she had some papers that someone would pay very dearly to get their hands on.'

'How dearly?'

'She said it would be enough for her to set herself up in comfort somewhere. And that if I were to marry her, she would even be able to clear off my debts and have enough left over to buy a cottage and lead a good life somewhere.'

'Hmm. That does sound a bit farfetched.'

'Would this be a good time to cut in and say, I told you so?'

'Never mind that. The pieces of the jigsaw are beginning to fit. You probably don't remember now but you mentioned it in passing to Adam that you had an idea that your troubles would be over soon.'

'Did I? I don't remember doing that.'

'It was on the way back from your encounter with the thugs at Marbury Arms.'

'Oh, that! Of course I was pretty disturbed after the incident. Yes, now that you mention it, I may have said something like that in passing to him. After that god awful episode, I had seriously started considering her offer, mind you.'

'Coming back to Summer's tempting offer to bail you out of your financial mess, what else did she say? Did she say how she was going to go about it or who she was intending to fleece?'

'No. All I know is that she had found these papers amongst her late mother's things.'

'Did she tell you what these papers were? A birth certificate perhaps?'

'No, she probably would have spilled the beans on the evening of the day you arrived but we were interrupted before she could. And later, I didn't get a chance to ask her. She was murdered soon after that.'

'So yesterday you went looking for something, anything that would resemble the incriminating papers she had talked about and found nothing.'

'You were there! You searched with me. There was nothing in that house.'

'Tell me, did you have something to do with Hogan's absence from the cottage yesterday?'

'Yes, I gave him ten bob the day before and I knew that would keep him out of my hair and out of the cottage for the day. Knowing him, I was quite sure that he would lose no time in passing it on to the closest pub keeper.'

'It must have been disappointing for you, the way the search turned out.'

'Best ten bob I've ever spent. Lesson learnt. Besides, I reckon Summer probably just dangled the proverbial carrot under my nose to get me to marry her. She probably lied about it all anyway.'

'Or perhaps not. Perhaps she did try using those alleged papers for a spot of blackmail and it got her killed.'

Chapter
Twenty Three

Rachel was back in her room. Her conversation with Neville had only served to bolster her belief that there was more to the tin of photographs than met the eye. And now she knew why Summer had hidden it. If she could not read, perhaps this was what Neville had been inadvertently looking for. If so, it would be a classic case of missing the wood for the trees. She was not completely sure as yet but she had a strong hunch that somehow the contents of the tin were the key to solving this mysterious case. As she pulled open the desk drawer to get the tin out for a second look, Betsy entered and informed her that Jeremy had just returned from the village and was requesting her presence downstairs in the study.

She hurriedly closed her desk drawer and went downstairs. Entering the study, she found Jeremy, Chief Inspector Harrow and three other men from the local constabulary.

Rachel greeted Harrow, 'Well, this is a pleasant surprise. The roads are open again, then?'

Harrow replied, 'Not quite. I got to Snodsbury by the milk train and took a farmer's horse cart rest of the way. Awful bumpy ride through the snow.'

'You have my sympathies, Chief Inspector. And, Jeremy, you are a dark horse. You never told me that you knew he was arriving today.'

'I didn't know, darling. The lad from Marbury Arms came in the morning with the message from the local constabulary that the he was expected to arrive at the inn. I couldn't find you...'

'Yes I was probably down in the servant's hall having a chat with Ivy.'

'Right, so I left a message with Hobbs and accompanied the lad back to Marbury Arms in his trap. By the way, allow me introduce you to Inspector Evans and Sergeant Pearce. You already know PC Downs.'

'Pleasure to meet you gentlemen.'

The two officers touched their hats in acknowledgment and Harrow spoke, 'The reason I was in a hurry to get here is two-fold. The first being that I do have some good news. I had word from the hospital that Lord Marbury managed to survive the second attempt on his life and I wanted to convey the same to his anxious family.'

'Oh that is good news. Hobbs, would you mind requesting the Countess to join us?'

'Certainly, madam.'

Harrow continued as the butler left. 'Secondly, my men did not find the birth records you requested at the London birth registry but the good news is that Sergeant Pearce did find one set of birth records at the local parish, after we received your telegram and you both were right - it may help in solving this case.'

'I see, so it can't have been Ada Cellini's son's birth record?' Rachel asked.

'I'm afraid not. We did run a check on her as well but there is no record of Ada Cellini having been in England prior to 1927, when she performed for the first time in one of Cellini's productions at the Old Vic. The first British legal document we could trace was her marriage to Donald Clayton two years later, in 1929 followed the same year by her son's legal adoption papers, in which Clayton adopted her son, who was five years old at the time. She must have given birth in Italy or someplace else. We have no idea if the father was Cellini or not.'

Rachel shook her head. 'No, Cellini could not have been Andrew's father as that would make him completely Italian by birth and Madame Cellini has driven it rather forcefully home to us, ever since the poor boy got here that he is half English. So the father must have been English.'

'I'm afraid there are no records to support that assumption. We have however found the girl, Summer's birth recorded in the local parish records. In absence of a father's name and occupation, the mother's name and occupation are given. I am sure you will find both quite interesting. Although the first name is smudged in places, the last name is clear and the occupation is given clearly as domestic service at Marbury Hall.'

At that moment, Miranda and the Countess walked in and a round of greetings followed to interrupt the Inspector's revelation. As the two ladies were brought up to date the Inspector continued.

'I'm afraid, all the entries in the parish records were written by hand, and the handwriting is none too legible.

Rachel and Jeremy peered over his shoulder as he read it out, 'The letters after M are not clear but I think it the last letter of the first name is either an "e" or an "a", which could mean that it says Marge Simmons, perhaps shortened from Margaret Simmons.'

The Countess took the paper from him and said vaguely, 'I don't know of any Margaret in service here at Marbury Hall but our housekeeper's name is Martha Simmons. Do you think it could be that?'

Miranda exclaimed, 'By golly! Are you suggesting that our prim Mrs. Simmons is Summer's mother? What a hoot!'

Harrow replied, 'Looks like it, and we now have the evidence to prove it. I suggest you ring for her, Lady Marbury and let's get this matter sorted once and for all.'

'Certainly.'

Five minutes later, the prim housekeeper walked into the room. If anything, Rachel thought she looked even more starched and grim faced than before.

The Countess informed her that the Inspector had found further evidence in the case and wanted to question her.

Mrs. Simmons nodded. 'I'd like to help if I can, milady.'

The Inspector confronted her point blank with the record from the birth registry.

She stood in shocked silence and then looked at him pointedly and said, 'I think you will find, sir that you have made a mistake. You see, I have never been married and in logical progression of that fact, I have certainly never had a child.'

'Not married? But I am given to believe that you go by the name of Mrs. Simmons.'

'Well, yes but surely you must know that all housekeepers and cooks in great establishments such as this are always addressed as "Mrs." as per tradition.'

Harrow shook his head unbelievingly, 'No, as a matter of fact I didn't know that. Are you quite sure?'

Mrs. Simmons responded with a touch of irritation in her voice, 'Well, of course I am sure. Why, our cook - Mrs. Meade has never had the privilege of being walked down the aisle either and we all address her as Mrs. Meade! It's just a tradition in the great houses like this one, that's all.'

Harrow looked flummoxed and said feebly, 'Right that could be so, but are you quite sure you have never given birth?'

Mrs. Simmons' mouth fell open and then she regained her composure and said in a clipped voice, 'I think, sir, I would be quite capable of remembering such an event had it been a part of my life and I am also certain that it would not have gone unnoticed in my thirty years of service here, considering that I have never taken more than a week's holiday in any given year.'

Harrow looked flustered and mumbled, 'Quite so, quite so.'

Jeremy smiled inwardly at Harrow's discomfiture and addressed Mrs. Simmons directly, 'Thank you Mrs. Simmons. As you said, we may have made a mistake. I apologise. You may go but could you please request her Ladyship's maid to present herself here. I believe her name is Tilly.'

As Mrs. Simmons left the room with her nose in the air, Jeremy explained to the others, 'I suddenly recalled that during the course of this investigation I did come across another woman in this house, who carries the same surname – Simmons, and I believe the name of the mother on Summer's birth record will match hers. You see, if I am not mistaken, Tilly's full name is Matilda Simmons.'

There was a hush in the room as Jeremy's words began to sink in.

Chapter
Twenty Four

Fifteen minutes later, a sobbing Matilda sat on the edge of a high backed chair in the study, surrounded by the police and her employers and confessed that she was indeed Summer's mother.

The Countess was flabbergasted, 'Why didn't you tell me, Tilly? In all of these years. I could have helped you.'

'How could I, your Ladyship? I was scared I'd get the sack once the baby started showing, being unmarried as I was. So I left the house and went away to stay with relations. Made up a story about wanting to work at a factory.'

'Oh dear! That explains why you left me to go away eighteen years ago!'

'That's right, milady. I am right grateful that you took me back after I had settled my little girl in with the Hogans.'

Harrow cleared his throat, 'Ahem, that's all very well but we are trying to find the link between the murders and we believe that your daughter, Summer, may have been killed to prevent her from disclosing who her real father was.'

Tilly's eyes opened in surprise. 'That can't be. She never knew who her father was. Nobody did.'

'I'm afraid you will have to come clean about his identity now, if you know what's good for you.'

'I can't. I promised him that I'd take the secret with me to my grave.'

'Look here, Miss Tilly, if you don't cooperate with us, I don't know about the grave, but you might just have to take your precious secret to the gallows with you.'

Tilly looked panic stricken for a moment before she started sobbing again.

Miranda spoke, 'Really Chief Inspector! Is this necessary? I'm sure hounding the girl like this can only...'

Harrow boomed, 'I will not have any interference from anyone, thank you. I have a murder and two attempted murders to solve here and I am losing my patience. Now, miss I'd like the name of the father, if you please.'

Tilly shook her head and looked up defiantly at him, 'I'd rather go to the gallows, sir than break my word to a gentleman.'

Just as Harrow looked as though he was about to suffer from an aneurysm, Rachel walked up to him and whispered something in his ear. He looked at her contemplatively and then nodded in agreement.

Rachel turned to the Countess and asked, 'May Tilly and I be excused? I think she is suffering from shock. Perhaps I'll take her to my room and give her some tea. I'm not sure she will be able to face a lot of people for the moment, either here or in the servant's hall.'

'I think that's an excellent suggestion, my dear. I'll have some tea sent up to you.'

Ten minutes later, Rachel had accepted the tea tray from Betsy and closed her room's door behind her, as the girl left. They were quite alone. She poured a cup for Tilly who was seated on the chair near the desk. She looked haggard.

'Did I tell you that I liked your daughter? She was very nice to me in her own way,' Rachel said gently as she handed the steaming cup of tea to Tilly and sat on an armchair facing her.

Tilly nodded, 'That is kind of you to say so, madam.'

'What was she like as a child?'

'She were a beautiful baby, so pretty with all that golden hair. Libby doted on her.'

'It must have been difficult for you to see her grow up so close by and have to keep a secret like this from her.'

'It was, madam but the truth would have broken her heart just the same.'

'But Tilly, were you never tempted to tell Summer that you were her mother? Not once in all these years?'

'Never, madam.'

'Could Libby have told her?'

'I made her promise not to and I do believe she kept her word, madam. Libby was a true friend till the end.'

'So you deliberately kept your distance from your own daughter?'

'I know you may think me heartless, madam but it were for her own good. And once she started working up here at the house, I kept an eye out for her, I did. She was a sweet girl but she had very little up there,' Tilly said tapping the side of her head with two fingers.

'That explains why you put the fear of God into Billy and the others, the day he reported he had seen Summer cavorting with Neville Pelham outside the gamekeeper's cottage. It wasn't to protect Mr. Pelham or Lady Claire's honour but Summer's!'

'Yes, madam. I fervently hoped and prayed that she wouldn't go down the same road as I did. I ticked her off every chance I got but now I feel terrible about it. She went to her grave hating me, I know she did,' Tilly said tears streaming down her face.

'You did what you had to, Tilly. What any good mother would have done and I am sure if she knew that you were her mother, she would have realised that you were simply looking out for her best interests.'

She sniffed into a handkerchief and said nothing.

'And another thing Tilly, you lied to the Countess just now, didn't you? About going and staying with relations because I very much doubt that you have any.'

'I am sorry, madam. You are right 'bout that but how did you know?'

'It's simple, really. You would have left Summer in their care if you had any, blood being thicker than water and all that. I think it was Summer's father who paid for your confinement somewhere comfortable and gave you a handsome sum for Summer's upbringing. You passed on whatever he gave you to Libby Hogan to bring up the child. Quite a rich man, isn't he?'

'Yes, madam.'

'And you aren't going to tell me who he is.'

'Not till my dying day. I owe him that at least, after all he's done for me and my girl. He didn't need to. One hears stories all the time about young unmarried girls in service with a bun in the oven, and nobody gives a tuppence for their plight. He did good by me and my girl and the least I can do, in return for his kindness, is to keep my promises to him.'

'And do you think that Lord Marbury is in any position to worry about your promises to him? Or perhaps you are holding on to the secret for the Countess' sake. You feel you owe her that,' Rachel said in all seriousness.

Tilly looked up and started laughing suddenly.

'Why are you laughing?' Rachel asked calmly.

Tilly spluttered through her laughter, 'You think Lord Marbury is the father! You think...you couldn't be more wrong, madam.'

Rachel smiled back and decided to play her last wild card. 'I know, I just wanted to make sure that he wasn't. You see, I've suspected for some time now. And I may as well tell you that I spotted a distinct resemblance between Baron Braybourne and your daughter, Summer. It was quite unmistakable really.'

Tilly's laughter died as soon as the words were out of Rachel's mouth. The maid's face went ashen and Rachel knew that she had struck gold.

Rachel continued blithely, 'Now that we've gotten that out of the way, I want you to think very carefully back to the day of Summer's murder. Did you know that the Baron was spotted near the laundry room around about the same time Summer was murdered?'

'No! Surely you can't think he had anything to do with that.'

'Why not? If Summer had somehow found out who her real parents were, would you honestly put it past her to make the most of her new found good fortune? A Baron for a father. It's like a fairy-tale come true for a penniless young girl, who has grown up thinking she was orphaned. Besides I distinctly remember seeing you coming out of his room the other night. Did you go in to check if you could find a blackmail note or something of a similar nature in his room?'

'No, madam. I was just packing his things for the hospital. You see, I know his preferences far better than that new valet of his. And besides, you are wrong about Summer. Even if she knew the truth, which I don't believe she did, Summer would have never blackmailed her own father. She wasn't like that, you have to believe me. And the Baron is a decent man. I've known him all these years. He has been kindness itself.'

'Oh, please! The same man who forced himself on an innocent young maid in the very house he was staying as an invited guest. I'd look up the Oxford dictionary but I don't think that the definition of "decent" even begins to fit a man like that,' Rachel said smartly.

Tilly responded calmly with shining eyes. 'I am sorry, madam. But it weren't like that and if you ask me, no dictionary will give you the truth of what happened all those years ago. This may come as a shock to you but nothing was ever forced on me. I loved him and he allowed me to love him. I am not ashamed to say it. I would look forward to his visits and count the days and hours till we could spend a few blessed hours snatched somewhere between dusk and dawn. I would have given my life to stay in his arms. I knew that was never to be. He is after all, a great man and I am what I am and I have never had any doubts about my station in life. Yet, when he found out that I was with child, he took me away, made sure I was looked after and gave me more than enough money to take care of my child. The only reason I came back to work here in this house, was so I could still see him every once in a while. I wasn't sure that I would ever see him again if I stayed anywhere else with the child. He was that sorry about our situation. After his wife died, God bless her soul, he never remarried. He still comes here whenever he needs comforting and I am there for him. So with all due respect, madam, you can take your dictionary and put it in your pipe and smoke it,' she concluded mtter-of-factly.

It was Rachel's turn to be rendered speechless.

Chapter
Twenty Five

Rachel walked down the stairs lost in thought after Tilly had left the room. She found her convictions being shaken off, like autumn leaves being blown away by a fierce storm before their time came. She could not shake off the sinking feeling that she had somehow lost her ability to see the truth. In all the previous cases she had solved, the truth had been revealed to her as surely as night turns to day. But in this case she had been wrong about almost everything. She had been wrong in her surmise that Ann Gibson was Summer's mother when clearly, her mother had been closer to home all along.

She had suspected that Summer had been blackmailing her real father, when her own mother was convinced that it was not possible. She had also been dreadfully wrong about the relationship Summer's real parents shared. She had jumped to conclusions about what had occurred in the past. She cringed inwardly as she berated herself for having read too many Victorian novels about the poor helpless maid ruined by the ruthless titled Lord. Real life was quite another kettle of fish. An eye opener, if anything. Who would have thought that genuine love and loyalty of the gentlest kind could have blossomed and stayed unshaken for decades between two most unlikely people, who walked in different worlds – a Baron and a lady's maid?

What about the connection between the soprano and the Earl? She had assumed that there was a connection between Ada Cellini and Lord Marbury and that Andrew was quite possibly the child of their union. The same child about which the Earl had spoken to the Baron about. But perhaps she was wrong about that too.

What about her conviction that the photographs she had found in Summer's room had a major role to play in this drama? Perhaps they were just Libby Hogan's family pictures with no further bearing on this case. She no longer knew if she had jumped to conclusions about Neville's innocence in Summer's death or even Ivy's innocence for that matter. Tilly's final outburst had made it clear that she could no longer trust her own judgement. She found herself grimacing as the question ran across her mind, 'How does one even begin to put a dictionary in a pipe and smoke it!'

She wondered what she would say to Jeremy and the Chief Inspector about Summer's father. She heard a distinct little voice in her head say that it wasn't her secret to reveal, just because she was privy to the information and had tricked Tilly into revealing the father's name. But then if Tilly was wrong and the Baron had anything to do with Summer's murder, withholding this vital piece of information could be disastrous to the case and her own credibility in the long run.

She decided that she would hold on to this piece of information for just another twenty four hours before sharing it with the others. From experience she knew that sleeping over conflicting ideas and decisions often brought her sparkling clarity by the time the sun rose. However, in this case, she wasn't even sure if she was making the right decision about sleeping over the decision!

Tilly was quite convinced that the Baron had no role to play in Summer's murder. But that was Tilly's view of the man she loved and knew well. A view that was also quite capable of being rose tinted. She wondered if it could be relied upon. On the other hand, if Tilly was wrong and the Baron was the killer, her own silence was akin to putting other lives at risk for another day. Rachel's thoughts were at war. She did the only thing she could do for now. She kept walking.

Still in a daze, she decided to take a detour through the long gallery and began crossing the huge dimly lit hall, her eyes gliding over portraits of the previous Earl and his ancestors. She had an uncanny sensation that their eyes were following her, watching her every move. She found herself thinking grumpily, 'I wish Adam would stop staring at me.' Before she could complete the sentence in her mind, she stopped in her tracks, retreated two steps and looked up at the painting. It was very much like a portrait of Adam, a paler, thinner and slightly older version of Adam. The brass plaque below it read, 'Magnus Pelham. The 11th Earl of Marbury'.

The light began to dawn.

II

She peeped into the library to see if Miranda was there, instead she found the Countess sitting alone staring into the fire. She looked lost and lonely. There was a glass of sherry on the table beside her. Her face reminded Rachel of someone else she had known, and it gave her a turn when she realised that the expression on the Countess' face resembled that of an Italian Madonna, surrounded by an aura of sadness combined strangely with piety and serenity.

Rachel treaded in softly, and as the Countess looked up, she took the armchair next to her without waiting for an invitation to do so.

The Countess said vaguely, 'Oh my goodness, is that the time? I must be off.'

She made a motion to get up and Rachel put her hand on hers and said softly, 'No, don't go just yet. Please. I know you want to be alone but I have something very important that I need to ask you. It won't take long.'

'Very well,' she said politely and sank back into her chair in a resigned manner.

Rachel asked gently, 'How long have you known that Adam was Miranda and Lord Marbury's son?'

The Countess looked uncertain at first, as though she couldn't quite decide how to respond to that but then she sighed. She turned to look Rachel in the eyes and said softly, 'From the day I first set eyes on him.'

'It must have been a painful recognition.'

'It was at first.' She gave a little laugh. 'You know the funny thing was that it took Magnus nearly three days before he realised but I knew long before he did.'

'Did you confront Miranda?'

'I didn't need to. I know what happened. You see, Magnus and I were engaged for two years before we were married. Miranda and I had been very close and it saddened me that in the beginning those two couldn't see eye to eye about anything. I used to love spending time in both their company but separately. I would dread his visits to our house. Miranda and he used to have flaming rows over everything, even the smallest of things. Towards the end of our engagement, a month before our wedding was to take place, Miranda and Magnus inexplicably fell in love. I'm sure it was as much of a shock for them as it was for me. But there it was. I thought of putting the wedding off.'

'So they did tell you about it?'

'No, they both thought they could hide it from me, but you see a woman always knows. We can sense these things even when there is no visible evidence of anything being wrong. Back then I could only surmise as to the extent which they took their secret liaison to. Adam's presence however, leaves no room for doubt now.'

'Hmm. What happened after that?'

'I waited patiently for either of them to confess but they didn't. So I thought I may have been mistaken. The wedding cards had been sent out and gifts began to arrive. By then two more weeks had passed and our household was in utter chaos, wedding plans were in full swing. Relations from different parts of England came to London for the wedding. Most of them stayed at our house and you can imagine how noisy and gay it all was. But amidst all that gaiety, I was miserable. I still thought that either Magnus or Miranda would come to me and ask for a release but nothing of the sort happened.'

'I see.'

At this point the Countess paused to take a long sip of sherry and putting the glass down, she continued, 'A week before the wedding, Miranda suddenly made an announcement at the dinner table that she had booked herself on a passage to Kenya, and that she would set sail right after my wedding. She said that she had had a letter from her old school friend – Felicity, who ran a mission in Nairobi. Apparently Felicity and her husband were in urgent need of extra helping hands at the mission and Miranda had volunteered. Our father was livid but Miranda had always been rather headstrong and finally our parents had no choice but to let her go. So, in the same week that I walked down the aisle to become Mrs. Pelham, my sister set sail to her new life of freedom, or so I believed back then.'

Rachel said nothing and the Countess finished the last of her sherry. 'If I had any inkling that she was carrying his child, I would have taken certain steps to ensure that she took my place at the wedding. But thinking back, I don't think Miranda herself knew that she was with child. Knowing her, I rather think that she was half way to Africa before it dawned on her that she was possibly experiencing something beyond plain old sea sickness,' she said with a wan smile.

At that moment Jeremy walked in, 'There you are! Chief Inspector Harrow and I were beginning to wonder what you've done with our suspect.'

Rachel spoke, 'Tilly is no more a suspect than I am, but I think you will find her in the servant's hall.'

The Countess said, 'More importantly, I think you had better ask the Chief Inspector and the others to join us here. I'm afraid, I have a confession to make.'

Chapter
Twenty Six

Chief Inspector Harrow took the written statement of confession from the Countess and requested Rachel that she call the others to the library. Rachel took the steps two at a time as she went upstairs to call the others. She met Andrew coming down the stairs.

'Whoa! Steady on, Rachel! Where's the fire?' He asked with a smile.

'The game's afoot, André!' She told him tongue-in-cheek and informed him that the Chief Inspector had requested an audience in the library.

'Let me go and fetch Mother from the sitting room. Won't she be pleased, this is just the sort of drama she enjoys!' He said, throwing a mischievous smile in her direction, as he went downstairs.

Rachel reached the landing and suddenly she was thunderstruck. She couldn't believe she hadn't spotted it before. She closed her eyes and stood still. Suddenly in her mind's eye, all the pieces of the puzzle began floating about her as though in slow motion and started falling into place, one by one. She had had an epiphany! And finally she knew who it was. The one person who had a clear motive to commit all five crimes. A ruthless and manipulative killer. And this time she had no doubt whatsoever that she was absolutely on the right track. She knew that she had some basic evidence to back her theory. She could have danced with joy as she had the growing conviction with every passing moment that it was the only thing that made sense, and tied all the crimes together until the realisation hit her that while her theory was sound in every way, she still needed a way to prove it!

Ten minutes later, she had composed herself and joined the others in the library where everyone had gathered. She had one last hopeful card to play and she had to ensure that this person would be present, waiting on call when the time came. She walked up to Hobbs and said something to him in a low voice. He nodded and left the room.

Chief Inspector Harrow spoke. 'Now that we are all here, I'd like to announce that the case has been solved and that we have a confession from the guilty party. Lady Marbury, would you like to say something?'

Rachel nodded in encouragement at her. Lady Marbury was serene as she spoke up in her quiet way. 'I think the time has come for me to do the right thing and tell you all that I shot my husband. And that I have just given a written confession to the police.'

Several voices spoke up at once.

Lady Stephanie shouted, 'Mama! That's not true!'

Baron Braybourne said, 'Yes, it can't be! What were you thinking?'

Lady Claire was too stunned to speak.

Neville stared about wildly and said, 'What on earth?'

Roderick looked bewildered, 'I don't believe it!'

'Santa Maria! I knew it was you!' The last statement was spoken with venom by Ada Cellini.

As the cacophony of voices died down, the Countess said with finality, 'Whatever you all think, it is true. It was me. I shot Magnus.'

Suddenly Miranda laughed and said, 'Nice try, Catherine. You couldn't shoot a sitting duck from ten paces! Chief Inspector, it's me you want. I'm the crack shot here. Ask Adam, ask anyone. I shot Magnus.'

Adam looked puzzled and shook his head. 'It couldn't have possibly been you, Aunt Miranda. You were with the others when I heard the shot.'

Miranda snapped at him, 'Stay out of this, Adam!'

The Countess spoke in a beseeching tone, 'No, Adam is right. It was me. Miranda, please. It can only be set right this way, don't you see?'

'No. It can't.' Miranda snapped back.

The Countess lost her patience and hissed, 'Do you really think I'd let you suffer any more?'

'Oh, goodness don't be such a drama queen. I can take care of myself, thank you!'

'I wish you could! Anyway the deed is done and I've confessed and that's all there is to it. Let's not have any more nonsense!' The Countess said as she regained her composure once more.

'If you think that I'm just going to stand by and let you take the blame for me, you had better think again! Chief Inspector, the confession is false and with all due respect if the police had any sense, they would know that my sister couldn't possibly hurt a fly.'

Chief Inspector Harrow looked at the bickering sisters and shook his head in disbelief. Rachel, who was standing next to him, heard him mumble, 'It's a bloody mad house!'

Rachel spoke up clearly and addressed the sisters, 'Never mind, which of you two ladies shot Lord Marbury, I'd be more interesting in knowing which one of you murdered Summer and why?'

Suddenly both the Countess and Miranda had a blank look on their faces.

Rachel nodded, 'Hmm. I thought so.'

Then she turned to look at the Chief Inspector and asked, 'May I?'

He shrugged and said, 'Go ahead, and if you can make any sense of any of this, be sure to let me know.'

She addressed the room.

'You see, they don't know why they killed Summer for the simple reason that neither of them did, nor did they have any role to play in Lord Braybourne's poisoning or for that matter, in Lord Marbury's shooting. This has been by far the most baffling case I have ever come across. I couldn't make the connections between the five crimes myself till about fifteen minutes ago.'

'You mean three, surely?'

'No, Chief Inspector, there were five crimes committed in and around Marbury Hall. The first victim was the gamekeeper's wife – Libby Hogan. Yes, I am quite sure now that her alleged accidental death was in fact wilful murder and a carefully planned one at that. The second was Lord Marbury's shooting followed by number three, Summer's death and number four, Lord Braybourne's poisoning and finally the fifth crime was the second murder attempt on Lord Marbury's life.'

She paused to nod at Hobbs and at her signal he went out and returned with Tilly in tow.

'Tilly, I am glad you are here. I need your help in identifying the people in these photographs,' Rachel said as she opened the tin box and spread out five pictures on the reading table.

Tilly came forward and said, 'Why, yes they're pictures of Libby and her brothers. A fine family they were. Came from good fishing stock.'

'Can you tell me who the girl in this picture is?' Rachel said pointing to the picture of the two young women.

'Aye, that is Libby's sister-in-law, Ann standing next to Libby. She was the one that sent Libby's poor brother, Toby to an early grave, she did. A good lad he was too.'

'Can you tell me more about her? Who was she exactly?'

'I can't say I know all the details, just what Libby told me.'

'Yes. Go on.'

'From what she said this girl was taken in by the Marsh family after her father died. Ann's father had saved her own father's life in the first war so he felt he owed him. But as they got older, Ann was a wild one and later she got involved in one of those music hall things and Libby and her fell out. The real trouble started when Libby's brother Toby married Ann. Libby was furious but he brought her around by telling her that Ann had promised to change her ways and that he was in love with her, and that she was going to have his baby. About a year after the baby was born, Ann took the baby and ran off with some theatrical gent or the other. It broke his heart alright. He went in search for her and the baby but it was no good. Libby said he had turned into a mad man, he became obsessed about finding her. He lost his job, took to drink and spent whatever he had saved traveling to London every other week, to look for them. She was nowhere to be found – like she had vanished into thin air along with his child. He started drinking heavy like and six months later he killed himself.'

'Thank you Tilly, you have been most helpful. You may take a seat now.'

Tilly went and sat in the far corner as Rachel spoke, 'Like everyone else in this room, not to mention the simple fishing folk in these pictures, I too was at sea, up until I realised that the truth was really quite simple and staring us in the face the entire time. On that note I have a question for you, Lady Marbury.'

'Yes?'

'Who gave you the information that the bloodstained blue silk dress of mine, found in the laundry room had a Schiaparelli label?'

'Why, I can't remember now.'

'Never mind. Let me know when you do remember. You see a while ago I met Andrew going up the stairs and he said something to me – that "this is just the sort of drama she enjoys" and that is when it occurred to me that this case has been exactly that – a carefully stage managed and meticulously planned drama, and one doesn't have to look too far to know who the main dramatis personae are! In this case quite possibly singular unless her son was a part of it, which I doubt. Isn't that right Madame Cellini, or should I say, Miss Ann Gibson? Or perhaps, you would prefer to be called Mrs. Toby Marsh?'

Ada Cellini spoke with incredulity written all over her face, 'Are you quite mad? Santa Maria! What have I got to do with any of these silly English people?'

Rachel mimicked her, 'Oh, ze silly English people! How you hate all things English, non? Reminds me of a line from Hamlet – "The lady doth protest too much, methinks." You did well and played the most extraordinary role of your life but I'm afraid you can't run from your past anymore.'

'This is slander! Chief Isspetore, you must arrest this woman. You cannot let her get away with such slanderous accusations against a world famous soprano like me!'

Rachel retorted, 'Really, you can drop your Italian accent now. As Tilly put it, I know you come from good sturdy fishing stock from Brixham.'

Madame Cellini bellowed, 'How dare you!'

Rachel hissed back, 'You never thought that you would run into a ghost from your past while performing at a grand place like Marbury Hall, did you? And Libby, your old friend, how she must've hated your audacity. Parading about as a Grande dame, an Italian soprano when she knew you were about as Italian as her toenail. What did she do? Threaten to expose your lie, sell your old pictures to the tabloids, and give them the sad story of how you ruined her brother's life, as a bonus?

'This is vile! Somebody stop this mad woman!'

Jeremy spoke, 'I say, Rachel are you quite sure?'

'Yes I am. Come and look at the pictures. André is in fact very much an Andrew and happens to be a spitting image of his English father, don't you think? Just look at that smile. And I suspect if she washes all that theatrical makeup off her face, we'll clearly be able to see her resemblance with the girl in this photograph. After all, Libby did when she came face to face with her here. And probably threatened to expose her for who she was, and I suspect that is what got her killed. And then the others...'

Miranda got up. 'Oh my God! Let me see that!'

The rest of the people in the room stood up too and as they walked towards the reading table, Ada shrieked, 'No! All of you, get back. Those pictures are mine...I mean...I mean...they are fake and a bloody malicious plot to sully my name!'

They all looked up at her in astonishment. She had finally cracked under the stress of Rachel's accusations. The Italian façade had broken and the last line was spoken in a perfectly ordinary British accent.

Suddenly Tilly screeched and attacked her like a fury, 'You witch! You killed my daughter!'

It took three men to separate the two women and keep Tilly from further harming Ada.

Harrow shouted, 'That's enough of that!'

Ada's hair was dishevelled. Her face was scratched and bleeding. She touched her face in disbelief and then turned and ran out of the room as though a banshee was on her tail.

PC Downs and Sergeant Pearce ran after her.

They all waited patiently for her return.

The Countess spoke up, 'Oh my God, you are right. It was Ada who told me about the dress being a Schiaparelli.'

Rachel nodded. 'I thought so. And she would have had no way of knowing that unless she had seen it herself in the laundry room when she attacked Summer.'

Chief Inspector Harrow asked Rachel, 'How on earth did you know it was her?'

'At first I didn't. The picture of Toby Marsh seemed very familiar. I knew I had seen that smile before yet to the best of my knowledge I had never met anyone by that name. You see once it came to me that Andrew had the same smile, I realised that he was Toby's son and working backwards on that connection, the odds favoured the idea that Ann Gibson was his mother and by default only one person could fit the bill – Ada Cellini. I then knew why she had to silence Libby and after her, Summer. You see, although Summer wasn't too bright, I think she managed to figure it out and tried to blackmail her.'

'I can understand how she could have murdered Libby but how did she manage to kill Summer in the laundry room? Someone would have spotted her in the servant's passage surely!'

'Ada Cellini was a soprano but first and foremost she was truly a great actress. The fact that she could pull the wool over people's eyes for so long in itself is stupendous. She was a master at theatrical make up. It was no big feat for her to steal a maid's apron and disguise herself as a maid and follow Summer into the laundry room and do the deed. Nobody notices people in uniform really. And in a house such as this with a large number of maids, she took a chance that no one would spot her. She just chose her moment well. As for the poisoning the brandy, which was indeed intended for Jeremy and me, I realised that she was the only one who could have easily manipulated the belladonna concentrate and framed poor Ivy for both crimes.'

Adam spoke, 'But I could've sworn that the nurse I saw at the hospital was a man!'

'Yes! That was sheer brilliance on her part. She added bushy eyebrows and layers of padding and thick stockings to act the part. She knew that she would be spotted in a busy hospital and someone or the other would be able to give a description. No one in their right minds would think of relating that description back to her.'

Roderick asked, 'What about shooting Lord Marbury? Why did she shoot him?'

'I believe Lord Marbury was very fond of riding about on his estate and on the day that Libby died, he saw or heard something suspicious and perhaps even saw her in the vicinity. He may have wondered what she was doing there and may have even questioned her, and she had no other option but to silence him but this is just pure conjecture on my part. We have no way of knowing that it's true until either of them tell us what really happened.'

At that moment they all heard a scream and a sickening thud.

'What in the blazes was that?' Chief Inspector Harrow asked.

They all filed out into the hall to investigate.

They found PC Downs huffing and puffing as he ran down the staircase and ran past them shouting. 'Terrible tragedy, sir. She's gone and thrown herself off the bally roof! Sergeant Pearce is still up there hanging on to one of the chimneys. Will somebody please go and help him!'

Chapter
Twenty Seven

The next evening, the headlines of all evening editions screamed different things. Rachel and Jeremy were sipping tea in the sitting room of Marbury Hall with the Countess, Adam, Neville and Baron Braybourne when Miranda walked in accompanied by Lady Claire and Lady Stephanie.

Miranda tossed a paper in disgust on the table and said, 'Have you seen this? It says – "Famous soprano plummets to her death. A tragic loss." Tragic my foot! The only tragic part about it was the way she cheated the hangman.'

The Countess spoke, 'Don't be unkind, darling.'

Rachel spoke. 'Speaking of headlines, mine is slightly more creative – "Marbury Hall's curse of death", and it goes on to talk about the 5th Earl's ghost being the main suspect behind these mysterious deaths.'

Lady Claire deadpanned, 'From what I've heard, the 5th Earl was supposed to be quite a mild mannered fellow, that is of course till one fine day, he went completely mad and decided that chopping his wife's head off was a jolly good thing to do!'

Jeremy smiled, 'We all have days like that. Lucky for most chaps, the feeling passes.'

Rachel laughed, 'Jeremy!'

Roderick spoke, 'Why Claire, you have my curiosity piqued. Tell me! What happened to this 5th Earl?'

'His sons locked him up in the tower wing and threw away the key to avoid scandal, and that's where he lived for the remainder of his life. Apparently no one knew he was dead until a funny smell, which was attributed to bad drains, was finally traced back to him.'

'Charming!'

'Tosca in life and death!' Baron Braybourne said, picking up another paper.

Lady Stephanie sighed, 'You know, if it wasn't for her murderous streak, I'd say her life's story would have been rather inspirational, even romantic. A poor English girl from a fishing village going on to become one of the greatest sopranos! She couldn't have possibly faked her talent. I wonder why she faked her identity.'

'I can tell you that.' A large man stood at the door. 'And I'm possibly the only person left who can provide you with the missing pieces of the puzzle.'

Baron Braybourne spoke up, 'Donald, old chap, good to see you. Very sorry for your loss. Everybody, I'd like to introduce you to an old friend of mine, Donald Clayton – Ada's husband and Andrew's father.'

There was a hush in the room.

The Countess was the first to speak up, 'Of course, you've come down for the funeral. Where are you putting up?'

'At Marbury Arms, and I've come by to collect my son.'

Miranda spoke. 'Andrew refuses to come out of his room after the shock he's had.'

The Countess said gently, 'And you must stay here for his sake. I can't imagine sending Andrew out, at a time like this. There are probably reporters crawling all over the place. Please do consider staying with us.'

'That is very kind of you, Lady Marbury but I have left my things at my room in Marbury Arms. I wouldn't want to impose on you.'

'It's no imposition. We have plenty of room and I shall instruct my chauffeur to go and get your things.'

'Well, I seem to have run out of excuses. After what has happened, it is extraordinarily kind of you to make this offer and I accept gratefully.'

'Whatever happened involved Ada and Ada alone. It does not reflect in any way on you or Andrew.'

'You are so kind.'

Rachel spoke, 'I'm glad you are staying. I'm Rachel Markham, by the way, and this is my husband Jeremy Richards.'

'I have heard of you both. Never imagined that we'd meet under such circumstances. The Chief Inspector told me that you were responsible for unearthing Ada's secret.'

'Yes but we are still foggy about so many things. Perhaps you could help us.'

'I am at your service. What do you want to know?'

Rachel asked, 'Her talent was her ticket to fame and fortune. The world would have still applauded her for that. Why did she have to reinvent herself as an Italian?'

'Apparently it all started as a lark. To understand that I need to give you some background. You see Ann Gibson did have a golden voice and her raw talent was spotted quite by chance by the great Cellini when she was performing at Sadler's Wells. From there on, he decided to take her under his wing and train her voice. So he whisked her away to Rome along with her son and arranged special lessons in music, acting, deportment, Italian language and of course last but not the least, he introduced her to the nuances of opera. Within two years she was his star performer and he married her. Finally he changed her name from Ann to Ada and the great soprano that the world is grieving today was born.'

'Sounds rather like a Roman version of Pygmalion.'

'It was. When she came to England to perform at Covent Garden, none of her friends or old acting colleagues even recognised her. She was moving in quite a different league of performers by then and all they could see was the great Italian diva, who also happened to be the great Cellini's wife. They assumed that she was Italian by birth and it tickled her fancy to let them go on thinking that. By then the media had turned her into an international star and there was no way for her to undo anything. Besides, she enjoyed the role. She once told me that she thrived on it and played the part, both on and off stage, to such perfection that she became another person.'

'When did she tell you all this?'

'Just before we got married. She told me all about her past. She had always wanted to be an actress and she had performed few bit roles in musicals before she was married. All that came to an end when she found that she was pregnant and she married and settled down to domesticity. You see, her first husband, the man she had been married to before Cellini had been a drunkard. He was a fisherman and would go out to sea for days, and on his return he would drink himself silly and leave her black and blue. She only found the courage to leave him the day he started hitting Andrew, who was just a one year old child at the time. She knew she had to save herself and Andrew from him and she did. She ran away to London and found work as a stand-in for a lead actress in a new musical. On the opening night the lead was taken ill and she got to perform. Fortune favoured her when Cellini spotted her on the opening night and offered to change her life. It was all too good to be true. Only it wasn't. She feared that she had made the same mistake by marrying Cellini, who according to her, was just a slightly more suave and sophisticated version of her ex-husband.'

Miranda said with cynicism, 'Touching but how do you know that story wasn't yet another fabrication of her imagination?'

'No, I knew that was true. Behind all the glitter, I knew Cellini was a slave driver and he was brutish with her, even in public, at times. In the eyes of the world she was a great diva but I saw the other side of her too – the lonely and frightened young girl. She came to me once or twice after they had had one of their violent rows and I felt dreadfully sorry for her and her young son. Finally Cellini died of a heart attack during one of their rows and after a decent interval I proposed to her. And before you begin to delude yourself that my motives were as pure as the driven snow, I must remind you that she was a great star and I am a businessman. I very much doubt that I would have made a similar proposal to a two bit actress given the same circumstances. The arrangement worked for us perfectly – I gave her freedom and a safe haven from all the brutes in the world and she shared her stardom with me. The fact that I became terribly fond of Andrew in the process was an unexpected bonus. It turned out to be a win-win situation for all of us.'

'Dad?' Andrew was standing in the doorway. 'I thought I heard your voice.'

'Come here, son.'

As the two men embraced Rachel found herself thinking that how odd it was that without fail, there were always two sides to every story.

Epilogue

Rachel, Jeremy and Betsy returned to Rutherford Hall after the inquest. Most of the details of the case were never made public. The men from the Foreign Office made sure of that. No one wanted an international episode. As one of the men said to them in complete confidence, 'The truth must never come out. It would be in our nation's best interests to keep it all very hush-hush and we must make sure it stays that way. It simply wouldn't do to sully the name of a great soprano and one of "Italy's National Treasures", as the newspapers put it.' Ada Cellini was given a grand funeral befitting her name and fame. The event was covered by the international press.

Betsy was the happiest to be back home and to Jeremy and Rachel's incredulity, she had a mystery of her own to relate. She told them that on the last night of their stay at Marbury Hall, she had heard the distinct sound of someone wearing leather boots walking about on the floorboards outside her room. Bolstered by the fact that the murders and attempted murders had been solved, she opened the door confidently and went out on to the passage and shouted – 'Hoy! Who goes there?' She could see a man in medieval costume with a feathered hat and riding boots, standing ten feet away. As he turned to look at her, she noticed that he was surround by a pale silvery light, and her hair stood up on end.

Suddenly he began walking towards her, his boots making the same sound that she had heard before. Being rooted to the spot in sheer terror, she couldn't move. Betsy said the form passed right through her and disappeared. She said that she couldn't stop shaking. When she recovered her voice, she screamed for help and all the maids came out of their rooms. Mrs. Meade had been kindness itself. She told her that the 5th Earl's ghost was an old fixture and never harmed anyone and then she made her a hot cup of cocoa to steady her nerves and offered her a spare bed in her own room for the night.

Rachel asked Jeremy later if he thought there was anything to that story and he responded with an amused laugh, 'I daresay, Betsy dreamt it up. A lot of people do have the most realistic dreams, you know.' Rachel shook her head and said, 'Yes, but how can you explain her being in the passageway, if it was just a dream?' Jeremy shrugged it off. 'The girl probably sleepwalks. All those ghost stories in the servant's hall just played tricks on her mind, that's all.' Rachel was not convinced. She had known Betsy long enough to know that the girl had plenty of courage, and for her to be shaken up like that was indeed an unsolved mystery.

Three months later, they received a telephone call from a joyous Countess who informed them that her husband had come out of coma and was back home again. To celebrate his homecoming she was throwing a weekend party – 'It's just family and the closest of friends. Do come. Magnus would be so pleased. He's still a little dazed about the events around the time of the shooting but I am sure he would love to meet you both. He has already heard so much about you from all of us.'

Rachel and Jeremy did go for the weekend and had a wonderful time reconnecting with all the people they had met earlier. They met Lord Marbury for the first time and he was both humorous and charming. Donald and Andrew Clayton were there too and Rachel was pleased to see that Andrew was looking happy and well again. Lady Claire and Neville Pelham were playing the 'perfect hosts in making'.

Lady Stephanie and Roderick came up to them, and excitedly informed them that they were going to announce their engagement over the weekend. Baron Braybourne jested that he was seriously contemplating a move to South America just to avoid the hassle of planning their wedding!

Later, the Baron took Rachel aside and thanked her for not revealing his and Tilly's secret. Rachel told him that it had never been hers to reveal in the first place, and since it had no bearing on the case, she had felt that bringing an intensely private matter like that, out in the open, would not have helped anyone.

Jeremy and she were introduced by the Countess to newer faces as well. 'Lady Astor has been dying to meet you. And oh, Mr. Churchill specifically asked for an audience with you both. He's in the library with some of the others. Come, it is best not to keep him waiting. He can be quite tetchy at times!'

While walking towards the library Rachel asked after Miranda and Adam. The Countess replied, 'Oh didn't I tell you, they left for Kenya last week. Adam is all gung-ho about setting up his new safari project. Magnus has bought a rather large coffee plantation and given him the reigns to run it. They will be operating the safari from there as well. I can just see Miranda toiling away on the farm, and enjoying every minute of it.'

On the last day, the Countess informed Rachel that she had been invited for a special tea given in her honour in the servant's hall. Rachel duly went downstairs at tea time and was greeted warmly by the staff. Billy brought her a bouquet of wildflowers tied with a ribbon and Ivy presented her a gift wrapped package. 'It's from all of us, madam'. Rachel was touched by their warmth. She spent half an hour with them discussing different things – from the weather to the latest motion pictures. She congratulated Ivy on her promotion to head housemaid. Taking her leave, she thanked them one by one – Mr. Hobbs, Mrs. Simmons, Ivy, Myrtle, James, then Bill Hogan, she shook Tilly's hand warmly and then complimented Mrs. Meade on her excellent scones.

Back in her room she put Billy's wildflowers in a vase and on opening the package, she felt close to tears. They had presented her with a beautiful silk scarf that must have cost them a pretty penny. Rachel felt humbled and honoured by the gesture. She had shaken Winston Churchill's hand. During the course of her two year career, she had met royalty and heads of State, and received expensive gifts and lofty praise. But to her mind, the silk scarf was the finest affirmation that she was on the right path and had chosen her career well. She knew that she would wear it with utmost pride – like a badge of honour.

Made in the USA
Las Vegas, NV
29 June 2022